THE DEAD LETTER OFFICE

GILLIAN ST. KEVERN

To Baxter and Maisie,

For making the editing of The Dead Letter Office go super fast by only allowing me a very small window of time in which to work...

Thanks for all the shenanigans!

Jasper ran his fingertips over the stiff card of the envelope. "Feel the quality. Either the letter emanated from the upper echelons of society or our correspondent is desirous of creating the impression that it does. Then there's the handwriting."

He held the envelope close to the gas lamp above his desk. Buried in the basement of the post office, the Dead Letter Office had been an afterthought—and no thought at all had been given to its lighting. Jasper beckoned his companions closer. "The many unnecessary flourishes indicate an infrequent correspondent. Observe the discolouration in the ink. Between writing the name and the address, our writer was interrupted. Our letter was set aside, rediscovered, and posted at a later date."

Nora crossed her arms over her chest. "I resent your inference that the writer was a woman. Plenty of men have hopeless handwriting."

Jasper beamed. Nora wore her thick black hair swept off her face in a serviceable bun. Her modest navy gown's red collar and trim echoed the uniform of their colleagues in the delivery service. Most suitable—as was Nora herself: punctual, practical, and particular. True, she was not as subservient as was desirable in a departmental junior, but Jasper saw no harm in allowing her to speak her mind. Nora's observations were to the point.

"True, my dear, very true. The majority of letters in our office back you up. However, the quality of the paper, the fact the letter was not sent promptly—and the mere fact of its arrival here—all point to a society hostess juggling the demands of managing her household, her family, her social engagements and her correspondence. Then there is the final, most damning evidence of a casual letter writer." He turned the envelope over, revealing the bare card. "No return address."

His companions echoed his sigh. Baxter and Nora had been in the Dead Letter Office long enough to share Jasper's feelings on the carelessness of those who omitted the return address.

"There is no street in London called Trafalgar Place." Baxter's shoulders slumped. "I tried Trafalgar Square, Trafalgar Avenue, Trafalgar Road—they all came back 'not known at this address.'" The scarring that marred Baxter's face exacerbated his mournful expression, giving a permanent droop to his mouth. His quick thinking when confronted with the letter bomb saved the lives of his colleagues. However, his resultant countenance was considered off-putting to the general public. Baxter received a medal of bravery and a demotion to the Dead Letter Office. He'd been there five years.

Jasper shook his head. "Not Trafalgar Road. The quality of the envelope! No—we must look closer to home. Our solution is in the writer. A harried society woman pressed for time might confuse our nation's great naval victories. Substitute 'Waterloo Place' for 'Trafalgar Place' and I fancy your envelope will find its home."

"Of course!" Baxter took the letter with a grin. "Thank you, Mr Carruthers."

Jasper chuckled, polishing his eyeglasses on his vest. "Always pleased to be of service." He glanced at the clock. "You've got just time enough to catch the afternoon mail."

As Baxter turned away to scribble the corrected address, Jasper gathered up his own pile of readdressed letters. He placed them in the metal canister that protruded from one brick wall. Nora added her handful, and Baxter thrust his envelope in with them. Jasper closed the canister, placed it in the pneumatic tube, and pulled the lever. It shot up the chute and disappeared from sight, making its way through the labyrinthine turnings of the General Post Office to one of the sorting offices.

Jasper shuddered. "Call me old-fashioned, but I don't think I shall ever get used to that. Ah, well. Baxter, you're on afternoon tea duty today, are you not?"

Baxter grinned. "I've got something special for us today." He ducked into the closet where the gas ring was kept.

"Now that sounds promising." Nora pushed the pile of letters on the sorting table to one side, making room for the tea tray.

"I hope you have not gone to any great expense." The afternoon teas were a tradition Jasper had instigated and the high point of his working day. He nudged a packing crate out of the way and drew his chair up to the sorting table.

"None at all." Baxter set down a plate containing three thick slices of gingerbread. "My mother remembered how fond you were of her gingerbread the last time she made it, Mr Carruthers. With her compliments."

"Why, this is splendid!" The gingerbread was a rich brown and generously buttered. A far more welcome sight than the rock-hard biscuits Nora produced. "You must tell her how much we appreciate her thought."

Baxter produced the teapot, Nora poured out, and the three of them settled down to the afternoon ritual.

"Speaking of mother," Baxter said, after they had appreciated the gingerbread down to the last crumb. "She wonders if there is any game about to reach its retirement date?"

Jasper glanced up at the row of pheasants, rabbits and turkey dangling from the ceiling. The misplaced game had given their office its ignoble name but had its own perks. "There is a pheasant, postmarked Kent, that I am sure will remain unclaimed. You must sign for it and—"

"If the owner makes a claim, substitute a bird of equal value. I know." Baxter set his cup of tea aside and took up a wooden pole with a metal hook on the end, used to raise and lower game from the ceiling rack. "This one? He's a good-looking bird. Someone surely regrets his loss."

"Poached, no doubt, from one of the finest establishments in the land." Jasper's brow clouded, remembering the illegible scrawl that had accompanied the wrapping paper. "Restoring it would cause the owner more embarrassment than its loss."

"It's an utter disgrace." Nora bumped her teacup down on the table. "The resources of this country hoarded by those with the least need for them! We have enough wealth to feed every man, woman, and child in Britain—but it is in the interests of those in power to keep us hungry."

Nora showed no signs of starvation. If anything, she verged on overfed. "Was there a meeting last night?"

Nora nodded. "The Lambeth Socialist Movement. It was well attended. And the speakers!" Her blue eyes shone. "You could not hope to hear a more complete rebuttal of everything wrong with our society."

"No doubt," Jasper agreed, "but you must be careful not to air your sympathies outside this office. Her Majesty's Postal Service takes a dim view of socialists."

Nora snorted. "They've already relegated me to the Dead Letter Office. What more can they do?"

Jasper shook his head. "You've got a promising career in front of you. Baxter, too."

"I've been here two years. Baxter, five." Nora scowled at the table. "To say nothing of your long service—"

Baxter blanched. "Ix-nay on the ong-lay."

Such dear children! Jasper smiled. "The Dead Letter Office suits me well. I am comfortable here and have not sought an alternative station. Our new postmaster will surely recognise your potential." He glanced at the clock. "On that note, we should get back to work. It would not do to be found at leisure."

As Baxter cleared the tea things away, the lift rumbled. Soon, squeaking wheels indicated Robinson and the mail cart were on their way.

Jasper held open the door. "What fresh delights have you brought us this afternoon, Mr Robinson?"

"Christmas has come early, Mr Carruthers." Robinson was a burly Yorkshireman who flung mail sacks around as though they were pillows. He heaved two large sacks into the office. One he tipped onto the sorting table, sending a wave of mail splaying across the desk's surface. The second he leaned against the wall.

A packing crate remained on the trolley. Jasper sized up the battered wood and the faded shipping labels. "I fancy we've seen this one before."

"Not known at this address. A rare failure, Mr Carruthers."

Jasper placed his hand on the box. "I remember now. Found on the Rotheram line with no label and no return address. Nothing but a torn scrap of an address label. O-U-R-T—Court. The only residence with 'Court' in its title on that line is Foxwood Court. Not known at this address, you say? I was so certain…"

Robinson clapped him on the back with such force that Jasper was almost propelled off his feet. "Don't take it to heart, man. Happens to the best of us."

"Even so…" Jasper removed his eyeglasses and took his handkerchief from his vest. "Put it beside my desk, if you will, Robinson. I shall rectify this."

"Right you are, sir." Robinson thumped the crate down with a carelessness that made Jasper wince. He beamed at Nora and raised his bowler. "Looking lovely as always, Miss Conway."

She rolled her eyes and ignored him, as she did every afternoon.

Unbothered, Robinson touched his cap to Baxter. "Pleasure to see your smiling face as always, Mr Lea. Like the sun emerging from behind a cloud, it is."

Baxter snorted but smiled all the same. "Take the comedy act somewhere else."

Robinson grinned at him and nodded to Jasper. "The postmaster general is making his way through the ground floor. Wouldn't wonder if you're next."

Jasper nodded, tugging his vest and tie straight. "Appreciated. See you tomorrow, Robinson." He turned to his staff. "Your cuffs, Baxter! Do you have a spare shirt?"

Baxter grimaced. "Are they so bad?"

"If you stand with your hands behind your back they will not be noticeable. You look very smart, Nora. If you could look more welcoming—" Her habitual scowl grew increasingly hostile. Jasper cleared his throat. "I daresay that will be sufficient." He took his seat and reached for the nearest envelope. "Let's look industrious."

A few minutes later, they heard footsteps on the basement stairs. A grimace passed between Jasper's juniors. He pretended not to see it, affecting great interest in the letter before him. As the door opened, he rose to his feet with an exclamation of surprise. "Postmaster Raikes! Mr Lea, Miss Conway, rise please—the postmaster general has favoured us with a visit."

Raikes was a thin man, albeit one with a great expanse of bushy brown beard and an ecclesiastical air of long-suffering. He nodded in return to the bows he received. "Afternoon, all. I don't mean to interrupt. I am acquainting our new postmaster with the General Post Office." He motioned the young man at his side forward. "May I present, Mr Nigel Carruthers."

Nigel stepped forward, his brown eyes levelled at Jasper in challenge. "How do you do." Nigel sported the Carruthers' jaw. He had a thin mouth and a lean, hungry look about his brow. His handshake resembled the press used to perforate stamps.

Jasper suppressed his grimace with difficulty. "How do you do." He motioned to his juniors. "This is Mr Lea, distinguished both by his diligent service and his considerable bravery. And Miss Conway, an adept assistant who has already mastered our ways in the short time she has been with us."

Nigel glanced around the office, taking in the game hanging from the ceiling, the stuffed pigeonholes, the filing cabinets, and shelves of itemised sundry items too large to be filed. He sneered. "It appears your ways leave something to be desired, Mr Carruthers."

Jasper's throat tightened. His chest tingled, as though oppressed by a great weight.

Raikes looked up from his contemplation of a portrait of the Queen at her coronation, postmarked Brighton, undeliverable. "Mr Carruthers and his staff have done wonders reuniting misplaced mail with their rightful owners."

"Nonetheless," Nigel continued, "I mean to make improvements here—as I do elsewhere within my post office."

"Commendable," Jasper murmured. "We look forward to any such improvements Postmaster Carruthers cares to make."

Nigel bowed his head in the slightest mark of acknowledgement, following the postmaster general from the basement.

Jasper forced a smile but discovered his muscles protested. "Well. Now that is over, we can return to work."

Nora and Baxter remained standing, staring at him.

"Carruthers," Baxter repeated. "Any relation?"

"My son." Jasper picked up the letter on his desk. "Now if you don't mind, we have mail to be getting on with."

He was aware of the glance that passed between his juniors, but neither of them asked any further. Baxter returned to his desk, Nora to hers.

Jasper turned over the envelope in front of him, barely taking in the water-stained envelope or the smudged ink. Nigel, a postmaster—and postmaster of the general office! A promotion any young man could be proud of. And yet, he did not think it was ordinary ambition that propelled him to seek such heights…

A warm weight pressed against his ankles. Jasper reached down, running his hand across a furry back. The cat arched into his touch, butting its head into his hand. He scratched its ears and picked up an envelope.

A few letters were still visible. Mr Br———e Esq. Ha——— —wns. He glanced at the pencil mark showing the postal route and reached for his ordinance maps. Hampstead Downs? No, the name of a house—there was no street by that name. Perhaps there was some clue to the letter writer's identity within.

The staff of the Dead Letter Office were the only of Her Majesty's Postal Service permitted to open mail. Jasper preferred to avail himself of this privilege as little as possible. He scanned the letter writer's address at the top and signature at the bottom—badly stained by water, but there was enough there for a return address. Jasper replaced the letter within its original envelope and wrote the return address. He stamped the envelope with the seal of the Dead Letter Office and set it aside to be placed in the following morning's mail.

As he did, a thought occurred to him. He glanced under his desk, but the only thing present was the crate, set there by Robinson. Baxter and Nora were bent over their desks, absorbed in their mail. No sign of a cat anywhere. And yet he could have sworn he'd felt it…

Nerves. Jasper shook himself. The altercation with Nigel had shaken him. He picked up the next letter. It was addressed to George, next but one from the big house on Walford Street.

Jasper's shoulders slumped. Did people think the postal service miracle workers?

2

"Zero seven-hundred hours." The bedroom door rattled as Candy thumped on it. "Up and at it, Private."

Jasper buried his head in his pillow. "Go boil your head, you stuffed turkey."

The heavy thump of footsteps indicated that Candy was already well on his way down the hallway, inflicting his booming voice and too-hearty greetings on another unfortunate occupant of the boarding house.

"A pox on retired army officers." Tempting as it was to remain in bed, Jasper could not allow himself the luxury. Unless he was very much mistaken—and after forty years' service among the postbags, Jasper did not think he was— Nigel's visit portended changes in the General Post Office. He could not be at a disadvantage. "May your glass eye fall out and your gout return." That did not mean he couldn't vent his displeasure. "Silly old goat."

He sat up and swung his feet over the edge of the bed. The chill floorboards were a salutary wake up: as efficient as the jug of cold water waiting for him on the washstand. Jasper thrust his feet into his slippers (a discordant plaid commercial sample, postmarked Edinburgh, and destined for a firm five years out of business) and pulled his dressing gown around his shoulders. He drew the curtains, grimaced at the misty grey without—January in London would depress anyone—and set to work on his morning ablutions.

He emerged from his bedroom, his skin rosy from the cold water, beard combed into spic and span neatness, and dressed in his uniform shirt, vest, and trousers. Then, Jasper made his way down the corridor to the dining room.

Candy stood in the corridor, pocket watch in hand. "Up bright and early, what?" he bellowed. Like Jasper, his face was pink from the invigorating effects of cold water and soap. Candy had combed his wispy hair across his shiny bald dome and arrayed his stout form in a crisp suit. He never appeared in anything less than parade ground order.

Jasper supposed he should be thankful Candy only brought his medals out on special occasions. "Unfortunately. Good morning, Captain."

Candy rocked back on his heels, his glass eye fixed somewhere over Jasper's shoulder. It was a bright forest green, the colour of fresh grass. With effort, Jasper kept his gaze on Candy himself. "No rest for the wicked, as they say."

"I've often wondered about that." Jasper stepped back to allow Betty, the maidservant, to squeeze past with a tray of kippers. "If there's no rest for the wicked, does that make slothfulness a virtue?"

Candy blinked at him. His round face broadened into a grin and he cackled. "Ha!" His laugh resembled cannon fire, rattling the paintings in the hallway. "Slothfulness—virtue! That's very good, Carruthers. I must tell the wallahs at the club that, eh?"

Jasper grimaced. Candy wasted no opportunity to remind the rest of them that he was a retired gent who spent his days reliving his glory years at his club. "You'll have them rolling in their armchairs."

"Is the coffee ready?" The poet, who occupied the room

opposite Jasper's, sauntered down the hall. He'd thrown a dressing gown over loose-fitting pyjamas stained with ink.

Candy glared at him. "Letting the side down a bit, aren't we? I don't consider that passing muster."

The poet's upper lip twitched. "Just as well I'm not in the service."

He smelled of tobacco, gin, and something rancid. Jasper pressed his handkerchief to his mouth. "Captain Candy alludes to the fact that, as this boarding house caters to a mixed clientele, we have an obligation not to appear in the public areas in a condition that might cause any embarrassment to our fellow guests."

The poet shouldered past him. "You two old maiden aunts might have nothing better to do all day than stand around polishing your buttons, but I have a deadline to meet. Betty! Where is that coffee?"

Jasper's mouth fell open. "Really!" What outraged him more: the insult, or being lumped in with Candy?

Candy glowered after the man. "You impudent young knave! If you were in my regiment, I would—"

"Not worth it," Jasper interjected. The last time Candy and the poet had argued, the poet had flung his hands about, knocked over the teapot, and the housemaid had burst into tears. In the resulting confusion, the toast had been burnt and Jasper had barely made it to the office on time. "We should just be thankful that this time he remembered socks." He shuddered at the memory. The poet took no better care of his feet than he did his attire.

"You can't call that decent." Candy stomped into the dining room, not moderating his voice. "In my opinion—"

"Which no one asked for," muttered the poet, helping himself to coffee from the tureen.

"A slovenly mode of dress indicates a slovenly soul within." Candy puffed out his chest as he took his usual place at the head of the table. "An Englishman, by paying attention to his mode of dress, signals his adherence to those civilising influences that make our nation great."

Mrs Holloway, the landlady, simpered at the end of the table. "Good morning, Captain." Those already present at the table added their greetings.

Somewhat appeased, Candy consulted his watch. "Zero eight-hundred sharp. Let's dig in, shall we?"

Jasper sank into his seat with a sigh. Why did most everyone in the boarding hostel allow Candy to browbeat them into his idea of order? The poet raised his cup in ironic salute to the landlady and walked out the door. The medical students who despised Candy made it a point of coming down to breakfast late. But the Irish widow with her three children beamed at him.

The butcher's apprentice snorted. "Don't have much call for dressing smart in my line of work."

"That may be so, Colin, but your diligence and hard work show themselves in many other ways. Besides," Jasper winked at him, "I thought you looked particularly smart on your way to the Young Person's Social last week. A special someone in attendance?"

The apprentice looked both pleased and bashful and mumbled something inaudible.

"Nothing like a well-dressed man to impress the ladies, eh?" Candy slapped the table, making the cutlery—and the maidservant—jump. "You wouldn't believe it now, but when I was a lad, I cut a fine figure."

"You astonish me, Captain." Jasper regretted the tone of his words, but Candy was impervious.

"It's true. That was before I lost my eye. A sad time, that was—me and my regiment, stranded in the mountainous regions of the Afghan. Hard desert terrain, and the mountains—let me tell you about those mountains!"

Jasper had heard about the ambush before. He devoured his toast in neat, even bites, pausing only to wipe the crumbs from his beard. When he stood, Candy was still going strong.

Odious, conceited man. Any excuse to puff himself up! Jasper combed his beard once more, returned to his room to don his brushed jacket and polished shoes, and set out. His annoyance carried him through the morning fog. Candy did not realise what a laughingstock he was. And worst of all, he seemed to like Jasper!

"I have nothing in common with that—that blowhard." Jasper's shoulders tensed. "How dare I be compared to him. Anyone would think that I—that I *tolerated* the man!"

A street urchin looked askance at him. "Buttonhole, sir?" she asked, raising a tray of carnations.

Jasper pinched the bridge of his nose. He would not allow either the preposterous notions of a hungover poet nor the boorish assumptions of a military ass to cloud his morning. "With pleasure, my dear." He handed over his coin, pinned the flower to his jacket, and set off on his way, a bounce in his step. There was this much for Candy's wake-up call: he had enough time to stop by his favourite bakery to pick up elevenses and afternoon tea and still arrive at work early.

The General Post Office was already humming with activity by the time Jasper descended the stairs to the Dead Letter Office, though he still had half an hour before his starting time. Better too early than too late was Jasper's motto. He hung his coat in his locker, and fussed around the office, putting things in order. Another sack of undelivered mail had arrived overnight and was scattered over the sorting desk. Jasper made a pile of those missives that needed simple readdressing or had been swept up with the mail for a different route. The rest he set aside to deal with once the morning's mail had gone out.

Task accomplished, Jasper felt much more cheered. He set a kettle to boil on the little gas ring and went to settle himself at his desk with the first of the day's letters.

"My! What is this?" Mail was not the only delivery that morning. Jasper stared at the dead mouse on his desk with distaste. "Disgusting thing." At least the post office cat was doing its duty, but to have such unwanted evidence of that fact!

Jasper felt pressure against his ankles. He looked down but saw only the gleaming polish of his shoes. His imagination? He used the edge of a letter to knock the mouse into the rubbish bin.

The kettle shrieked as it reached boiling point. "Right on schedule." Jasper filled the teapot. A strong cup of tea would banish any imaginings. Jasper straightened his shoulders. If the pile on the sorting table was any indication, he'd need all his wits about him to deal with the day's mail.

3

Jasper's hunch was—as usual—correct. The seasonal boom in Christmas cards led to an increase in the amount of misplaced mail.

"Christmas cards might be a boon for our takings," Baxter grumbled, dropping yet another pile of envelopes into the pneumatic tube. "But I wish someone would think of us."

Nora snorted. "Cole thought all right—thought of how much profit he could gain at our expense."

"You can't deny it is a pleasant custom," Jasper remarked. "And doubtless a source of joy for those who enjoy it, though I'm not sure it will last. It seems rather faddish."

"A way to extort more income from those who can ill-afford to part with it, at the expense of those who cannot afford to object to the work? Oh, it will stay," Nora intoned. "I predict this is only the start."

Baxter looked around the office. "We need more staff. Not one sorting room upstairs has less than twenty clerks."

"We're cosy enough, the three of us," Jasper said. "I don't see how we could fit a fourth in here—let alone sixteen. There would be no room for the packages."

"We could petition for a bigger room," Baxter said. "Turn

this into a warehouse for the packages. Or reduce our holding time for non-valuables. Six months is rather generous."

"They tried that once," Jasper said. "During the civil war. It proved unpopular and was soon reversed."

"The civil war," Baxter repeated. "If the department hasn't been updated since then, it explains an awful lot!"

Jasper cast around for some distraction. He heard the thick crunch of Robinson's boots with relief and put his cup of tea down. "Goodness, is that the afternoon delivery already?"

Robinson had one sack and a message. "Postmaster Carruthers requests Mr Carruthers in his office."

So soon? Jasper cast a hasty eye over his uniform and beard in the teapot. "I must not keep him waiting."

"A bigger room," Baxter said. "And more staff."

Nora nodded. "Our pay does not reflect our work."

Jasper winced. The last thing he wanted to do was to rock the boat. "If the opportunity arises to pass on your suggestions, I shall. But I rather fancy that the postmaster has something else in mind."

The General Post Office was designed to impress the public with the majesty of the postal institution rather than rendering the duties of the postal service easier. Clerks bearing sacks of letters thronged its long corridors, hurrying from department to department, each step moving the mail closer to its ultimate destination.

The offices of the senior staff members were on the second floor, removed from the breakneck activity. A secretary held the fort in the waiting room outside the postmaster's office. He nodded in greeting to Jasper but continued to type. At length, he rose and glided into the office. When he emerged, he held the door open. "The postmaster will see you now."

Jasper murmured thanks and stepped into the room.

He could hardly imagine a greater contrast to the dank clutter of the Dead Letter Office. All was light and space, the generous window behind Nigel augmented by wall sconces holding gas lamps. Nigel's head was bent as he scanned the document his secretary had left.

Jasper waited in silence. This was deliberate. Nigel, even as a child, had done nothing without purpose.

Finally, Nigel looked up. "I wish to talk to you about the Dead Letter Office, Carruthers."

"I am all ears, Postmaster." There was a chair beside the desk, but Nigel had not indicated it. Jasper dared not avail himself—doing so was tantamount to admitting he was past it.

Nigel placed his hands together. "I've been looking at your last month's report. Your department is singularly inefficient. Although the quantity of mail delivered to the Dead Letter Office has increased, your output remains unchanged."

"The recent increase in mail is a seasonal fluctuation," Jasper murmured. "As we put Christmas further behind us, the amount of mail we have to process will return to its usual level. We will soon catch up with the excess."

Nigel looked at the report in front of him. "A sloppy way of dealing with things. I wonder how you have allowed things to reach such a point."

"We have added more staff to our department," Jasper protested. "Miss Conway has greatly assisted in the delivery of missent mail."

"She was hired two years ago," Nigel said. "You have not made another hire since then?"

Jasper grimaced. "There is considerable internal prejudice against working in the Dead Letter Office. Unlike other branches of the service, it offers few opportunities for advancement. We are out of sight, out of mind."

"A fact which no doubt explains why such lax behaviour has gone so long unchecked." Nigel narrowed his eyes.

Jasper continued as if he hadn't heard. "The time spent training the staff makes recruitment a slow process. Our staff do not learn one or two postal routes. They must be conversant with the entire country. Then there is the matter of finding people of suitable integrity. The Dead Letter Office is the only branch of the service permitted to open mail. This potential breach of privacy means we must be most particular in whom we employ."

Nigel sneered. "What would a man who abandoned his wife and child know of integrity?"

There was a rushing in his ears. Jasper stared straight ahead. His voice sounded at a great distance, even to himself. "There is a significant difference between my behaviour in my personal and professional lives."

Nigel stood. "You always cared more about your career than you ever did your family. Your years of long service and apparent devotion might have fooled your superiors in the past, but they won't fool me." He tapped the folder on his desk. "I know you are motivated by nothing more than self-interest, to whom loyalty is but a word. I promise you, I will find you out and I will have you dismissed."

Jasper's shoulders heaved as he breathed in. "The postmaster general must sign off on any dismissal. You will not find proof that will convince him. My record speaks for itself. I may not be satisfactory as a father nor a husband, but I am an adequate postal clerk."

"That remains to be seen." Nigel's eyes glittered. "Remember, I know you. I will find the proof I'm after. I advise you to prepare for your retirement now. You are dismissed from my office, Mr Carruthers."

Jasper bowed. "Thank you, Postmaster Carruthers."

Jasper was shaking as he left the office, so much so that he mistook his turn and found himself in Savings and Loans. Jasper stepped behind one of the great marble pillars, smoothed his tie, and straightened his jacket.

Nigel's words echoed in his mind. *I advise you to prepare for your retirement now.* He couldn't mean it!

Jasper swallowed. Nigel meant it, all right. He was determined. "But then again, so am I." Jasper's years of service stood him in good stead. He was punctual, had never quarrelled with any other departments, indeed, he prided himself on his affability. No one had any complaint against him—no one save Nigel.

Jasper frowned. If there was anything in his record that showed him in a bad light, Nigel would find it. In all his years of service, there was only one letter he hadn't delivered. If his son should uncover it—

No, Jasper told himself. *It was like looking for a needle in a haystack.* Nigel would exhaust himself long before he happened upon it. The greater danger was that his age should count against him. He was not as young as he once was, nor did he feel inclined to fight the battles necessary for the Dead Letter Office to achieve the place it deserved. Was Nigel right, and his presence a burden to the department?

4

"Well?" Nora demanded as Jasper stepped back into the office. "How did it go?"

Jasper removed his glasses, reaching for his handkerchief. He preferred not to see the disappointment on his juniors' faces. "I'm afraid I had no opportunity to put forward either your outstanding service or your suggestions for improvements. The postmaster hauled me over the coals for allowing this department to fall into laxity and idleness."

Baxter's cry of dismay sounded genuine. "Surely not, Mr Carruthers. Why, you're never idle! You're always first to arrive and last to leave."

Nora nodded. "And you've taught us so well. Your system of sorting the mail first saves us hours throughout the day."

"I'm afraid that I was not as energetic as I should have been in securing for our department the staffing it needs. I shall have to apply to the postmaster for permission to hire another junior." Jasper sighed. "However, I very much suspect we must prepare ourselves for even greater change."

"This is our chance," Nora said. "What greater moment than this to remake the department? We should be the instruments of this change, take control of it."

Baxter nodded. "It's plain to see that someone with no idea of the necessity of light for deciphering poorly written labels made the decision to house us down here."

"We're in the basement because the wisdom of the postal service decreed that it would not do public confidence—or private morale—any good to have before them evidence of the failure of the postal service to do its intended duty." Jasper shook his head, replacing his spectacles. "I'm afraid we must resign ourselves to our position here."

Baxter and Nora exchanged a glance. Baxter pulled a chair up to the sorting table. "It didn't seem right to have afternoon tea without you."

"Do you mean you waited?" *What dear children!* Jasper drew up his chair.

"It is your treat," Nora reminded him.

"So it is." Jasper bustled into the cupboard to make the tea. "I find it hard to go past a good cream bun—and if the biscuits we had this morning were any indication, these should be very good."

Afternoon tea did not remove the shadows the interview with Nigel had cast, but it did lift Jasper's spirits. He was competent at his job and, biased though he was, he did not think his personal failings warranted dismissal. No, he must travel hopefully, even as he braced for stormy weather.

Nora and Baxter had the newly arrived parcels in hand, so Jasper applied himself to the crate returned by Robinson the day before. He inspected the outside. It was papered with a curious mix of shipping labels. It originated in Egypt and had been transferred to a mail boat at the Suez Canal before it arrived in England. The railway label was there, as was the Dead Letter Office stamp—covering another label. Jasper peeled it off carefully. The label was that of an American-bound liner. *Two* American liners, in fact.

"Goodness." Jasper ran a hand over the label. "You have had quite the journey, have you not?"

"I beg your pardon?" Nora looked up.

Jasper coughed. "My apologies, Nora. I was talking to myself."

She glanced at the clock. "I hope you don't think me impertinent, Mr Carruthers, but the time…"

He looked up. "Ah, yes. You must get along. How are you going, Baxter?"

"I've almost finished this last letter," Baxter said.

"You may leave when you are finished." Jasper chuckled. "Class dismissed."

Nora threw on her coat and hat and flew up the stairs. Always in a hurry! No doubt a girl like herself had plenty of friends and plans. Even Baxter, whistling as he pulled on his coat, must return home to a warm welcome. His mother was his housekeeper and seemed proud of her son.

Jasper turned back to the crate. He had made his decisions, and he now lived with them. On the whole, it wasn't a bad life… There was plenty to interest him. This crate, for example…

A notation in pencil was scrawled across the second of the liner labels. Jasper noted it down and went in search of the records department. He found what he was after in the records of shipments received. Crate sent from Egypt by H. Wilson, return address, New York. Destined for—and Jasper permitted himself a smirk—Foxwood Court. He'd known it!

But if the address had been correct, why was the parcel returned? He turned his attention to the logbooks of the Rotherham mail route. Yes, there was the crate, received by the mail train. It had indeed reached its destination—only to be returned to sender.

"Hum." This was a most unlucky package! Jasper returned to the mail boat records. Yes, there was the crate again, returned to New York. And a mere week later, back on the mail boat bound for England—and this time to a P. Leighton at a London address.

Jasper noted the address down. It was all clear now. During its travels, the tag with the London address was lost, and the Foxwood Court label used to direct the parcel to an out-of-date address. Clearly, P. Leighton had moved in the interim. Mystery solved!

Returning to the Dead Letter Office, Jasper wrote up a fresh label for the crate and rang the bell for Robinson. While he waited, he put on his coat and hat in preparation to depart.

Robinson grinned as he saw the crate. "You've solved the case of the misaddressed case then, Mr Carruthers?"

"I believe so, Mr Robinson." Jasper patted the crate. "The intended recipient seems to have moved house while the package was in transit. I found the new address. There should be nothing preventing it from being delivered now."

Robinson grunted as he heaved the crate onto his trolley. "Bet they'll be glad to see it! Probably given it up as lost."

Jasper sighed. "It is a source of great sorrow to me that more members of the public do not avail themselves of our aid in finding their lost packages. Though, while you're here, I've been meaning to have a word to you about your cat."

Robinson paused. "My cat, Mr Carruthers?"

"The post office cat. I know that such an animal is very useful and a boon to our office, given the nature of some of our packages." Jasper motioned to the game. "All the same, I wonder if more care could be taken to tidy up after it. I found a dead mouse on my desk this morning. Not calculated to put one in a, shall we say, *productive* state of mind."

The Yorkshireman's snort was more amused than disapproving. "I'm afraid there's not much I can do to help. The post office doesn't have a cat."

Jasper blinked. "We don't? But—"

"You're thinking of Old Blackie," Robinson said. "When Grovenor retired—you remember him? The nightwatchman

—Blackie retired with him. Inseparable those two were. I hear he's thrilled with his new life as a house cat."

"Ah." Jasper studied Robinson. "But if we have no cat, how did a mouse end up on my desk?"

"I'm not saying we don't have a cat. But we don't have an official post office cat. I suspect a stray may have snuck in. Matter of fact, I thought I heard something mewing last night, but I put it down to imagination. Had a look, but I saw nothing."

"A stray," Jasper repeated. "We might put some milk out for it. If it proves to be industrious, perhaps we should keep it as a replacement for Blackie."

Robinson's eyes twinkled. "Would it be joining your department, Mr Carruthers?"

Had the news of his dressing down reached the sorting offices? Jasper winced. "If I remember rightly, Blackie chose his preferred department. Good night, Mr Robinson."

Jasper's custom was to return to the boarding house after work, where the landlady would have his meal kept for him. Tonight, however, he took the omnibus to Dove Crescent. He made his way to number eighteen, a spic and span little townhouse.

The maidservant who answered the door was crisply attired in an apron and cap. She looked at him askance. "Mrs Carruthers is not in the habit of receiving gentleman callers so late at night."

Jasper smiled and held out his card. "I'm an exception. Please let your mistress know I'm here."

Patience came herself to greet him. "Hello, Jasper. If I'd know you were coming, I'd have held dinner."

Jasper shook her hand. "This is just a quick visit. No need for any fuss. How are you keeping?"

Patience motioned him into the parlour. "Quite well, on the whole. Getting older, but one can't do much about that."

"You astound me. I should say you're not a day older than the last time I saw you." Patience's hair might have more grey in it, but her figure was still trim, and she moved like a much younger woman.

She waved him towards a chair. "Is it too late for a cup of tea?"

"I don't want to impose. I might scandalise your maid." Jasper paused. "She's new, isn't she? Evelyn didn't suit?"

Patience sat in her chair, picking up her knitting needles. "Evelyn has found herself a position in a much more prestigious household. Daisy is her replacement. I'm still training her."

"I am sorry to hear that."

"One expects it. If you hire a girl you pay less in wages, but you must train her. Inevitably, once she is trained, she finds a better situation."

Jasper frowned. "Is the cost of keeping a maid too much?"

Patience shook her head. "I enjoy training them. It gives housekeeping more of an interest."

"Then you're comfortable? Not in any need?"

Patience looked directly at him. "What's this about, Jasper?"

He squirmed. "I spoke with Nigel today. He gave me to understand that, in his opinion, I have, well… treated you rather shabbily."

"Ah." Patience's needles clicked as her fingers settled into a regular rhythm. "As our child, I suppose it's only natural that he takes an interest in the manner."

Jasper stared at the china shepherd and shepherdess standing on the mantelpiece. A wedding present. Patience had kept them in immaculate order. "I am not all that could be hoped for in the matrimonial department, but I thought we were ticking over all right."

Patience pursed her lips. "I have not complained." Yet,

something in her tone indicated that she had grounds for complaint.

Jasper glanced at her. "I did what I thought was for the best. You've got your own house, and I trust, an ample sum for housekeeping and expenses."

"I cannot deny that I am comfortable," Patience agreed. "All the same, I should have liked to have been consulted."

Jasper winced. "Perhaps I was peremptory... but at least we have had no serious disagreement."

"Yes," Patience agreed, still with that strange tone. "Lord forbid we argue."

Jasper cast her a suspicious glance, but her expression was blank. "You cannot prefer an unhappy marriage to our present arrangement?"

"Unhappiness takes many forms." Patience unwound her yarn. "Take Nigel, for example. He would have preferred an acrimonious relationship with his father to no relationship at all."

Jasper looked up, stung. "It was Nigel who decided he didn't want to see me any longer. I was grieved, but I respected his wishes. I still respect his wishes."

Patience's needles clicked. "Did it ever occur to you he might not have wanted you to respect his wishes?"

"You're saying Nigel wanted me to ignore him?"

"To fight for his regard," Patience said. "To show him you cared enough to stick around through the unpleasantness."

Jasper shifted. "No one would want to be miserable, surely. Always better not to rock the boat."

"That might work in the postal service, but there are some things in life one must fight for." Patience's expression clouded. "Your problem, Jasper, is that you've never fought for anything."

"Quite right. I abhor any kind of violence." Jasper nodded. "Harmony at all costs."

Patience's eyes rested on him. "Life is not a compromise."

"Nor is it meant to be a battle, my dear." Jasper stood. "I'll wish you a good night. If you need anything, you have only to write to me."

Patience remained sitting, her expression thoughtful. "I think it would do you good to fight for something."

5

There was no mouse on Jasper's desk the following morning, but neither was the plate of milk left out overnight touched.

"It appears the stray elected to find other employment, Mr Robinson," Jasper reported, as he wheeled the day's mail sacks into the office. "Good heavens—not again!" The crate rested on the trolley, just as Jasper had last seen it, with one change: the words 'not known at this address' scrawled across his printed label.

"Like a homing pigeon, this one," Robinson agreed. "Shall I put it on your desk?"

"Please." Jasper glanced at the clock. For the crate to have returned so promptly meant it must have gone out with the first mail—and the parcel coach driver might still be at his lunch. "Baxter, I'm going to visit Packages. I shouldn't be above a quarter of an hour, but in my absence, you're in charge."

Jasper located the coach driver, a flax-headed youth with a scattering of freckles. "Sure, I remember that package," he said. "Anyone would have thought I was trying to deliver a bomb! The gentleman what answered the door gave me a right earful. On and on he went. Hadn't he already indicated that Mr Leighton was unknown at this address? How many times was it necessary to send back the package before the postal service got the hint, or was this an example of our competency?"

"Oh, dear. I seem to have landed you in it." Jasper frowned. "He said it was previously delivered?"

The coach driver nodded. "Rum thing, that was. I reckoned he knew the crate. He turned as white as if he'd seen a ghost when he saw the package. And his tone with me!"

"Did you enquire if Mr Leighton had left a forwarding address?"

The driver nodded. "I will not repeat what he said, Mr Carruthers. It's not fit for your ears. The general gist was that Mr Leighton was not known at the address, had never been known at the address, and was not likely to ever be known at the address, so I should take my package and stow it—well, somewhere packages aren't likely to be stowed."

Jasper winced. "Some members of the public think paying their taxes gives one a licence to be rude. I can only say again how sorry I am, and that I was sure that it had not been delivered previously."

"Oh, I don't blame you, Mr Carruthers," the driver said. "You're only doing your job, ain't you? But I tell you, I ever see that toad-faced bludger when I'm out of uniform, I'll sock him one in his big fat nose."

For reasons of interdepartmental harmony, Jasper pretended he hadn't heard that. He returned to the Dead Letter Office, only to find it deserted. Neither Nora nor Baxter were at their desks.

Baffled, Jasper consulted his watch. It was early for elevenses, and neither of his juniors would leave the office unstaffed. What had happened?

He stepped through the partition that separated the public, when they cared to make enquiries, from the office, and almost tripped over Nora on her hands and knees on the floor. "Good heavens, Nora! What on earth are you doing?"

She scrambled to her feet. "I'm so sorry, Mr Carruthers. I was looking for the cat."

"The cat?"

"Here puss, puss, puss." Baxter crawled out of the pantry cupboard. "Mr Carruthers! I beg your pardon—"

"I grasp the situation." Jasper shook his head. "Return to your work. If the cat is desirous of making our acquaintance, it will let us know. In the meantime, we are representatives of Her Majesty's Postal Service. We must act with the dignity that post requires."

"Yes, Mr Carruthers," his juniors chorused, dusting themselves off.

Jasper sat at his desk regarding the crate. It seemed Mr Leighton had moved again. Clearly, he was a haphazard sort of chap. He must return the crate to its New York sender and hope they had a better idea of Mr Leighton's whereabouts than the residents of the London address.

Jasper hesitated to pick up his pen. Was this his usual reluctance to return to sender—or something more?

"Hang on." Jasper reached for his notebook, consulting his notes on the crate's long journey. *P. Leighton.* No sign of *Mr.* Had the man at the door made an assumption or was he subverting the delivery of Her Majesty's Postal Service? Perhaps he should inspect the crate's contents before sending on its long journey back to New York. "Baxter, my lad, I wonder if I could borrow you for a moment."

Baxter used the departmental crowbar to lever the lid of the packing crate off, revealing sand tightly packed around the contents within.

"It's from Egypt, all right." Jasper wrinkled his nose. "Nora, could I trouble you to stand by with the broom?"

Nora bristled. "Why am I asked to stand by with the broom? Baxter's got two hands, hasn't he?"

"I need Baxter's assistance lifting whatever is in here out so we can examine it." Jasper brushed away the sand, revealing smooth grey stone. "Here we go. *Heave ho!*"

At last, they placed the contents of the crate on the sorting desk. It was a compact grey stone statue depicting a sitting cat, its front legs stretched to their full length, its back legs curled either side, with its tail standing erect behind it. A carved collar surrounded its neck, with a hollow space in the centre, suggesting an ornament was once placed there.

"Egyptian, isn't it?" Baxter peered at it. "I've seen statues like this at the museum."

Nora scoffed. "I think you'll find it's a casket, not a statue."

Jasper looked at her with dismay. "Casket?"

"How many statues do you know of with a crack down their middle?" She pointed.

There was indeed a crack down the middle. The front of the cat lifted off to reveal a receptacle containing a small, linen-wrapped bundle, the head of which was painted to resemble a cat.

Jasper removed his spectacles, polishing them on his handkerchief. "I believe this is a departmental first! I feel like an archaeologist, don't you?"

Baxter peered at the bundle. "A mummified cat, no doubt. They used these as offerings to their gods, the ancient Egyptians did."

"A religious offering? That would make passing around the collection plate rather difficult, don't you think?"

Nora was not impressed with Jasper's joke. "Who on earth puts a mummified cat in the post?"

"H. Wilson, New York."

Nora was not diverted. "I'm not having this ghastly thing in the department. It's unsanitary."

"It's been in here for days already and no one's sick," Baxter protested. "Besides, powdered mummy is beneficial for the health. There was an auction of them just last month, wasn't there?"

"For fertiliser," Nora corrected him. "That's very different. And I'm not having that thing in the department."

"Calm yourself, my dear," Jasper said. "I shall copy out the inscriptions on the casket and see if we can learn anything more about it. Baxter, see if there's anything else in the crate —a letter, perhaps, something that might give us an insight into the owner's current whereabouts."

Baxter fished in the crate and discovered another dead mouse and a letter so mouse-eaten it was all but illegible.

"This is the problem with mail boats. They stow the packages in the hold and forget them until they reach the shore." Jasper dropped the letter fragments into a fresh envelope and labelled them with the delivery number of the crate.

"What do we do with all this sand?" Baxter looked at the floor.

Nora glared at them both from her desk.

"Sweep it up and place it in the crate," Jasper told him. "We may need it to deliver the cat to its rightful owner." He turned to Nora. "You don't object to us storing the crate here in the meantime, do you?"

She shuddered. "As long as that thing is in the crate with the lid on, it's all right."

A gentleman arrived just then, eager to locate a package intended for Whitehaven Road. Jasper set aside the cat and assisted him. By the time the package was retrieved and signed for, Baxter and Nora had departed for the day. Jasper noted down the crate's inscriptions and considered the hefty object. There was no way he was going to lift that lid without Baxter's help. No, it was most unorthodox, but he would have to stow the casket—cat and all—in his locker overnight.

As Jasper closed the locker, he felt a weight against the back of his legs. He smiled. "What did I say? The cat will introduce itself when it wants." He looked down, beholding his polished shoes and nothing else.

The pressure repeated, accompanied by a rumbling purr.

Jasper's head rushed. He heard a pounding noise, not unlike the crashing ocean. Gripping the locker handle for steadiness, he knelt, extending his hand.

His fingers brushed warm fur. The cat thrust its sleek head against his palm.

"My word." Jasper's legs failed him. He sank to the floor, his hands shaking.

This could not be happening.

A pressure on his lap. He saw the crisp fabric of his trousers crease beneath invisible paws as the cat kneaded him into a comfortable seat.

Jasper raised a trembling hand, felt again a furry body, heard again a rumbling purr. He shut his eyes, choking back a gasp. He had a horrible suspicion he knew why this package had gone undelivered.

6

Jasper arrived at the Dead Letter Office the next day to find a runner waiting for him with the message that Postmaster Carruthers wanted to speak to him at once.

The officious-looking secretary had not yet arrived. Jasper knocked on the office door. Should he feel proud that Nigel had inherited his father's punctual habits?

This time, Nigel did not make him wait. He sat at his desk, a form laid out on the table before him. "We've received a complaint about your work, Mr Carruthers."

Jasper kept his expression blank. "I'm sorry to hear that, Postmaster."

Nigel narrowed his eyes. He had his mother's eyes, clear, flecked grey and green like a forest creek, but with none of Patience's temperance. "Twice now, we have delivered a package to 14 Trent Street. How do you explain this?"

The mummified cat. Naturally. "The first time the postal officer was obeying the label on the package," Jasper explained. "He marked it 'unknown at this address,' and returned it to us, only the address it had been sent to was removed in transit. I discovered a label from an earlier posting and mistakenly directed the package back whence it came."

Nigel sneered. "I hope this is not an example of your work, Mr Carruthers. Did it not occur to you to check the shipping labels for the address?"

"I did, Postmaster Carruthers. There was no record that a delivery attempt had already been made. I assumed that the label had been lost before any delivery—"

Nigel waved aside his explanation. "This is not good enough."

"No, sir."

Nigel's eyes narrowed. "The public expects their mail delivered promptly and to the correct address. Errors damage the reputation of the entire postal service." His tone was short. Annoyed? Could Patience be right that Nigel wanted an argument?

If so, he was out of luck. "I quite agree. I intend to look into the matter further and locate the rightful recipient of the package."

"You had better find them," Nigel snapped. "I shall expect an update on this package—and I do not want the inhabitants of 14 Trent Street harassed again."

Jasper blinked. "Harassed. Was that the word chosen by the, ah, complainant?"

Nigel looked up. "What do you mean by that?"

Jasper stroked his beard, giving his next words full consideration. He did not wish to antagonise Nigel. "It just strikes me as a strong choice of words...considering the circumstances."

Nigel gave him a withering glare. "Your job is not to consider the circumstances. Your job is to deliver the mail. Dismissed, Mr Carruthers."

❧

Jasper was still sorting the mail when Baxter and Nora arrived. "I'm afraid that I'm not ready for you," he murmured. "I'm not myself this morning."

Baxter peered at him. "Coming down with something? You don't look like your usual self."

Jasper coughed. "A poor night's sleep. I had rather a strange dream." More like a living nightmare. He had been half inclined to not show up for work. Only the knowledge that, with Nigel in the postmaster's office, an unexplained absence was likely to result in instant dismissal had got him out of bed that morning. "You can divide this pile between you and make a start while I finish up."

As Baxter and Nora got to work, Jasper kept a covert eye on his juniors. Both appeared focused on readdressing their mail. Neither seemed conscious of a cat—invisible or otherwise.

Was it possible that he'd imagined it after all? Or had the thing departed? As Jasper sat at his desk, he felt a familiar pressure against his leg. He reached down with his hand. Whiskers tickled his skin, and the cat pressed its cheek against his fingers.

Not imagination. Oh dear. Jasper glanced up and saw Baxter watching him with a quizzical expression. He coughed and reapplied himself to his task. The last thing he needed was a rumour circulating that he'd lost his mind.

The cat leaned against his leg for some time and then settled itself beneath his desk. Jasper heard the crackle of wrapping paper as it settled itself, followed by a low purring. He saw Nora pause and look around the room, but she made no comment and he did not dare ask.

Mid-morning, the cat brushed by his leg on its way out from under the desk. Jasper did not guess its location until they paused for elevenses, and Baxter discovered the little jug of milk knocked over and a good amount of it lapped up.

"The stray must have returned. Look." He pointed to wet paw prints across the floor.

"I didn't see any cat," Nora said. "Did either of you?"

Jasper shook his head. "I thought I heard purring."

"Me too." Nora's frown increased. "It's a bold animal. Stealing milk from right under our noses!"

"I daresay it won't do us any harm to have our tea unadulterated for once," Jasper suggested. "I could do with a strong cup."

Shortly after their elevenses, Jasper returned from a trip to the records room to find Nora conversing with a member of the public. It went as Nora's interactions with the public so often went: downhill.

"I must have a name and address," Nora insisted. "It's standard practice not to discuss the mail unless we know whom we are talking to."

The man stiffened. "Your colleagues have twice attempted to foist my belongings off on someone else. To insist on identifying me at this late date seems irrelevant."

Jasper shut his eyes. He was tempted to turn on his heels before either of them saw him… But no, his conscience would not allow it. He took a deep breath, fighting the rise of nausea in his stomach. Wiping clammy hands on his jacket, he approached the quarrelling pair. "I'm Mr Carruthers, the head of the Dead Letter Office. Can I be of service, sir?"

The man turned to him. He wore a suit that was well made but which did not altogether fit him. He had a prominent bald skull, and his eyes were large and glassy-looking with prominent bulges on either side.

Like a toad. Jasper frowned. Why did that sound familiar?

The man glared at Jasper. "As I was telling this impertinent maid, I would like my property."

"Naturally." Jasper flicked open the record book. "And your name?"

"I fail to see why this interrogation is necessary."

Jasper gave the man his most disarming smile. "This department receives several hundred undelivered letters and packages a week. To identify yours, we need to your name—or at least, the name your package was sent to."

The man glanced around. "Leighton," he mumbled. "P. Leighton."

The mummified cat! Jasper paused. The mail coach driver had described the man who'd refused the parcel as a toad-faced bludger and announced his intentions of socking the man on his big fat nose... He directed his gaze to the man's olfactory organ. It appeared, in Jasper's opinion, to be outsized.

The man's scowl increased. "What are you staring at?"

"P. Leighton." Jasper glanced at the clock. The coach drivers should still be in the canteen. "I think I remember seeing a package addressed to that name. If you do not mind, I shall send my junior to locate it." He scrawled a quick note on a piece of paper and gave it to Nora. "You do not mind waiting? She won't be a minute."

Nora shot him a puzzled look but went upstairs. Baxter paused his work, recognising that something unusual was going on.

"Can you tell us who sent you the package?" Jasper continued, flicking through the record book. "It will make the process of identification much easier."

"No, I can't." The man looked around him again. "Is this likely to take long?"

"I'm afraid so. When mail can be delivered to the stated address, there is no need for identification. Being resident at the location is considered, if not proof of identity, proof one has the trust of the homeowner. Whereas, when one visits our department, we must ask for such details the parcel's recipient might be expected to know. Such as," Jasper continued, "how you came to know that we had a parcel for you, Mr Leighton."

"Why—the friend who sent the parcel told me."

"Splendid! And the name of that friend?"

The man blinked. "I—"

In the silence that followed, Jasper felt a pressure against his ankles. An audible meow followed.

The man's face dropped. He backed away, looking around him. "Get away from me you—you pestilent creature!"

Baxter stood, approaching the partition. "What is he talking about?"

Jasper held up a hand, motioning for Baxter to stand back. "I think Mr Leighton is confused."

"Confused." All the fight and bluster of moments ago had left the man. He was pale, a clammy sheen on his skin. "Yes. I'm sorry, I—I wasn't thinking."

"That's him!" The coach driver stood at the top of the stairs, Nora beside him. "The man that told me to take the package back! Mr Leighton not known at this address, eh?"

The man cried out in alarm and dashed down the corridor. The coach driver took off after him. Nora, never one to miss out on excitement, followed suit.

"We lost him," she reported later. "He must have taken cover in one of the side corridors and ducked out once we passed him."

"What on earth was he playing at?" Baxter wondered. "Denying the package twice and then turning up to claim it?"

"Some funny business," Jasper agreed. "I do not know who the man is, but I doubt that he is P. Leighton."

"What do we do?" Nora asked. "Report this to the Special Agents Office?"

Jasper nodded. "Yes." Just as well to record the incident. "I'll write up an account, and you'll both need to sign it."

Nora added her signature to his report without

complaint. "Who on earth would want to steal a dead cat? You couldn't pay me to keep that thing."

Jasper swallowed. And she didn't know the half of it!

"Collectors," Baxter said. "Egyptologists will pay a lot for a mummy in good condition, even if it is only an animal."

"Ghastly." Nora shuddered. "Why would anyone want a collection of dead things?"

Baxter motioned to the ceiling. "You know that you work in the Dead Letter Office?"

She pursed her lips. "One must draw the line somewhere."

Jasper interposed before things could get further heated. "It would be just as well to put the lid back on the crate, Baxter."

Jasper returned from filing the mail fraud report to find both his juniors departed for the day and the casket still in his locker. To his dismay, the crate had been sealed without the cat inside. He decided he had no alternative but to leave it where it was another night.

Fate had other plans. Arriving at his office the next morning, Jasper found a uniformed police constable taking the nightwatchman's statement.

What now? Jasper hurried over to join them. "Is everything all right, gentlemen?"

"Mr Carruthers!" The watchman beamed. "You're just the man that can help us." He beckoned the constable over. "No one knows the Dead Letter Office better than Mr Carruthers. He'll know at once if something's gone."

The constable gave him an appraising glance. "Reported burglary, sir. Your department door was observed to be left open, and the nightwatchman gave his opinion this is not the usual state of your office."

"Goodness gracious me!" Now that he was looking for them, the signs of trespass were obvious. "A trolley has been pulled through here—look how carelessly this stool has been left! Making for the storage, no doubt."

He hurried forward, scanning the shelves. Numerous valuables made their way to the Dead Letter Office. There was an entire map chest filled with watches, necklaces, rings, and other tokens, ranging from the sentimental to the extravagant. The thief had not cared for those, nor had he touched the fine china, bronze statuettes, or rare books.

"There was a crate here." Jasper pointed. "See the outline of the sand? It seems to have sprung a leak. Our thief placed it on his trolley and departed—yes, there is a trail of sand." The constable, watchman and Jasper followed the trail to the lift and from there to the back entranceway.

"This is a calamity," Jasper said. "Stealing from Her Majesty's Postal Service is stealing from the nation."

The constable frowned. "I'll report this to the station. We'll do our best to find the man responsible."

"Please," Jasper intoned. The toad-faced man was the likeliest culprit—and they knew his address. They only had to go to 14 Trent Street and arrest the man. And in the process, destroy the man's character and any chance of a career...

Jasper winced. What if he was wrong? He could not blight a man's prospects. No. He would say nothing. The report was there. The constable only had to look for it.

Jasper had the office tidied up before Baxter and Nora arrived and did not mention the burglary. Neither noticed that the crate was missing, and the day passed without further incident.

When Jasper was finally alone in the department, he opened his locker. The casket was there, undisturbed. As suspected, the thief had taken the crate, not realising its precious cargo was not within.

Jasper stared at the stone cat. To leave it at the post office was to risk it being stolen. But why not let the toad-faced man take it? He might not be P. Leighton, but it would solve the problem of the package. Nigel only cared that it was delivered...

No. Jasper shook his head. His allegiance was to the post. He would find the cat's true owner. Glancing around to make sure the office was empty, Jasper lifted the casket and dropped it into his trusty carpet bag. He pulled on his coat and his hat and marched out of the department. His heart beat fast. In all his years of service, this was only the second time he'd removed a piece of mail without signing for it. Stealing from the mail was stealing from the nation. And yet, his conscience would not permit him to do anything else.

7

The journey home was fraught. Jasper expected a constable around every corner, or worse—Nigel, a smirk on his mouth as he contemplated the success of his plan. When Jasper finally reached his room in the boarding house, he collapsed onto his bed.

He lay eyes shut, contemplating again the risk that he had taken. The mattress beside him dipped. Whiskers tickled his cheek and a furry head bumped against his chin.

Jasper kept his eyes shut. The cat was less upsetting when he couldn't see that he couldn't see it. "I must be mad." He dragged his hand across his forehead. "What have I done?"

The cat leaned against him, tail trailing across his face. Then, with a soft thud, it jumped from the bed. Jasper watched his bedclothes flutter as the cat crawled beneath. Exploring its new house?

He had a bottle of gin for special occasions. Jasper poured himself a glass and drank it neat. It made him feel somewhat better, so he poured himself another.

It was one thing to decide that he would see the cat to its rightful owner, quite another to do it. Now that the crate—cat and all—was, to the knowledge of the rest of the post office, stolen, he would have to be discreet in his investigations.

What was there to investigate? Jasper stroked his beard. The key thing was to locate P. Leighton. The obvious first step was visiting 14 Trent Street, but that risked tipping off the toad-faced man to Jasper's pursuit. No, 14 Trent Street must remain a last resort. So what alternatives were there?

The cat had evidently finished its explorations. Jasper got a moment's warning as a paw rested on his leg, and then a weight jumped in his lap. "I beg your pardon!" The cat kneaded him, preparing to settle itself. "Some warning would be appreciated."

There was a thump from the adjoining wall. "You called, Carruthers?"

Was there no limit to Candy's self-importance? To imagine that Jasper had anything to say to him! "Talking to myself I'm afraid, Captain."

"You've got to watch that," Candy bellowed back. "Catch yourself replying to yourself, you know you're in trouble, what?"

Jasper didn't deign to reply. The thin walls of the boarding house had a lot to answer for.

"I say," Candy considered after a pause. "I was just having a nightcap. Care to join me?"

"No, thank you," Jasper said firmly. "I've had a long day."

"Ah. Well. Another time, perhaps." The floorboard creaked as Candy moved away from the wall.

The cat purred. Jasper tensed, but there was no commentary from the next room. Was the cat audible?

He hadn't considered that. Jasper fondled the cat's ears. The landlady had a strict no-animal policy and had expelled boarders on such grounds before. He was risking more than his career. He looked around his room. True, the bedsit was no magnificent prize, only large enough to hold Jasper's bed, the washstand, his armchair, and a bookcase, but the rent was reasonable, the food adequate, and it was only a short walk to the office. No, he must not risk being cast out. He must find P. Leighton as soon as possible.

From the soft scraping sound, Jasper guessed the cat was cleaning itself. At least it was an orderly creature.

"Think." Jasper massaged his temples. What had Baxter said? The cat was likely to be owned by a collector, someone with an interest in Egyptology. He had copied the inscriptions on the casket. Could that aid in the cat's identification, and explain, if not merely who was likely to be interested in it, why a cat mummified centuries earlier was sitting on Jasper's lap?

That was the greater problem, Jasper decided. Even should he discover P. Leighton, would the man be willing to accept his parcel knowing that it came with an invisible feline?

Questions, Jasper decided, stifling a yawn, best left for another day.

The cat slept on his bed. It was still there the next morning when Jasper left for work. Although he listened out for it, he did not hear the telltale rumble of the cat throughout his day at the office, nor did he feel anything brush against his ankles.

Was the cat's presence linked to the vicinity of the casket? Jasper twirled a pencil. That would explain the dead mouse within the crate, though not why the mouse had destroyed the enclosed letter. Or had something happened to wake the cat? Jasper could not see an invisible cat going long unremarked on in the confined space of a ship.

Yes—there were possibilities there. He had not one, but three boats on which the cat had been a passenger.

Baxter raised an eyebrow as Jasper pulled on his coat. "Special occasion, Mr Carruthers? You're usually the last to leave."

"I'm not easy about that crate," Jasper confided. "I am going to visit the docks, see what I can learn."

"That is dedication to duty." Baxter shook his head. "What do you suppose you'll find?"

"I'm not sure," Jasper admitted. "But I should like to make the attempt." He frowned as he mounted the omnibus that would take him to the docks. This was a fool's errand, no doubt about that.

Only one of the boats was then in harbour, the American liner that had carried the crate back to America on its first unlucky journey. The ship hand looked askance at Jasper's enquiry and reported that there had been no strange happenings of any kind, nor any cats onboard. The stationmaster suggested that if Jasper cared to leave messages for the crew of the remaining boats, he would see them delivered.

Jasper returned to the boarding house, footsore, weary, and no further ahead. He ate the lukewarm dinner set aside for him, barely registering the food. The cold evening and damp atmosphere of the docks had a detrimental effect on his joints. He wanted nothing more than to collapse into bed with a hot stone at his feet.

It was not to be. Candy lingered in the corridor outside his room. "Ah, Carruthers. There you are! Join me for a tipple?"

Jasper eyed him with dislike. The man could not take a hint! "There is nothing I should like less. However, I am tired, so if you'll excuse me—"

Candy shook his head, grinning. "You're not getting off the hook that easily, no. You'll want to hear what I have to say."

Jasper paused. Candy was usually insufferable, but there was something different about his self-satisfaction today. He stroked his moustache with the air of a preening cat—

The cat! Jasper glanced towards his room. Had Candy discovered it?

Candy's grin increased. "The cat is out of the bag, as they say. You have no choice."

"I see." Jasper breathed out, trying to school his expression into order. He must not jump to any conclusions. He must find out how much Candy knew—and what he intended to do about it.

Candy's room was no bigger than Jasper's, crammed full of so many bits and pieces that it resembled a second-hand furniture shop. Candy fussed around, pouring two glasses of whiskey. "Could have knocked me down with a feather. Last person on earth I'd have expected to keep a pet—and right under our landlady's nose, too! You're a dark horse, Carruthers." He held out a full glass.

Jasper smiled thinly and took the glass. "It's only until I find the animal's rightful owner."

"That's what they all say." Candy splashed a generous amount into his own glass. His hand shook. Drunk already? He couldn't be nervous, surely. "I doubt you'll be able to part with it. Cats have a way of making themselves at home in a way that old bachelors like ourselves have little defence against." He gulped down his whiskey. "Ah, that's the stuff. A top-up?"

"No, thank you." Jasper took a sip of his drink. It was much better than he was expecting. Candy treated himself all right. "I assure you, I have every intention of finding the cat's home—though I would be obliged if you didn't tell anybody about it."

"Naturally." Candy toasted him waggishly with his glass. "The cat will be our secret." He contemplated Jasper with obvious satisfaction.

He was for it. Jasper's fingers tightened around his glass. He must take control of the situation. "What do you intend to do about it?"

"That depends on you." Candy rocked backwards on his heels. "I've had my eye on some rooms in Milton Street. Two bedrooms with a shared sitting room and all conveniences." He motioned around himself. "As you may have observed, my present situation is rather cramped."

Jasper raised an eyebrow. "Cramped is putting it mildly."

"Ha! True, true." Why on earth should Candy look pleased at that? "To get to the point, the rooms would suit me, but I'm in need someone to go in with me."

Jasper swallowed. A guilty man feeling the noose around his neck could not be more aware of his doom. "And you have decided that I fit the bill."

Candy nodded. "I've been considering the matter for some time. I was not sure that we'd get along, but the cat changes everything."

The cat gave Candy the upper hand. He had only to go to the landlady and Jasper's room would be searched, the casket found, and his ignominious dismissal from her Majesty's Postal Service would be a foregone conclusion. "I'm afraid I am rather busy at present. I don't know that I have time to move."

Candy waved his concerns aside. "Don't worry about that. I'll take care of everything." He beamed. "I am sure you'll find the rooms to your satisfaction."

Jasper swallowed a large mouthful of whiskey. "I'm sure I will." What other choice did he have?

andy delivered on his threat. In a matter of days, he'd shown Jasper the rooms, informed their landlady that her tenants were departing, and installed himself, Jasper, and their belongings in their new rooms.

Candy leaned back in his armchair, placing his feet up on the ottoman before him. "Much better than our last digs, eh, Carruthers?"

Jasper considered the room. The sitting room faced the street and had a good amount of sunlight during the day. Even at this time of night, the closed curtains and fire burning in the grate gave it a cheerful air. Candy's furniture and that supplied with the room more than satisfied their needs. Mrs Hollins, the landlady, a cheerful motherly sort, was tidying up the remains of their dinner: a hearty stew designed to ward off winter chills. "Indeed. My compliments, Mrs Hollins, on a most excellent repast."

She beamed, red cheeks glowing. "I'm glad. I used to be a cook, you know, and it makes a difference cooking for someone that enjoys it."

"Two someones, Mrs Hollins." Candy patted his ample stomach. "I shall have to pay a visit to my tailor soon. Ha!"

Jasper pursed his mouth in distaste, but Mrs Hollins didn't seem offended. "I'm happy to oblige with a pot of tea or a little something any time of day. And I don't mind putting the dinner hour back for you, Mr Carruthers."

Jasper almost choked on his glass of hot water and whisky. "Now that is unnecessary. Just put mine aside."

"Nonsense," Candy said. "A man who works as hard as you do needs a good hot meal. I don't mind waiting. Matter of fact, when I was in the service, I had to wait a good deal longer."

"The military?" Mrs Hollins asked. "You can always tell an army man by his appetite."

Candy twirled his sandy moustache. "I might not be on active duty but my stomach hasn't yet worked that out."

Mrs Hollins laughed and bustled out.

Jasper sipped his drink. The rooms were comfortable, the food good and plentiful, and the cost not that much more than his previous rooms. The other shoe must drop any moment now.

Candy set his whiskey down. "How's the cat?"

There it was. "Good."

"I haven't seen it."

And he was not likely to. "I'm keeping her in my room." Jasper's voice was strained. He coughed, attempting a casual tone. "I understand that, upon a shift in environment, a cat is liable to make a run for it. I do not want to lose her."

Candy nodded. "She got a name?"

"No." Jasper was not even certain the cat was a she. "I don't want to get too attached. No doubt her owner has already chosen a name."

"How did you come across her?" Candy stroked his moustache. "Don't tell me she was in the mail."

"She is not the first cat that I have encountered in my professional duties," Jasper said. "What the public deems mail-worthy would astonish you."

"Oh?" Candy brightened. "Sounds like you've got some stories there."

Jasper pressed his lips together. "Another time." What was Candy's game? Angling for lost property? He watched Candy pull out his newspaper, finding his place, apparently content. Did he not realise the hold he had on Jasper, that this was more than a case of sneaking a cat past a landlady?

"Dreadful thing, this Burr case. Hard to think of a child so young going to prison, but the crime…" Candy shook his head. "There's not been so vicious a murder since that Whitechapel business."

Jasper winced. "The least said about that the better. They still haven't caught the chap."

"And it's my thought is they never will." Candy shook the pages of his newspaper. "What the police force is coming to these days! They wouldn't stand for such incompetence in the armed forces, I can tell you that."

Jasper made a non-committal noise, looking into the flames. The last thing he wanted was a repeat of Candy's thoughts on military discipline.

Candy lowered his paper. "Pound for your thoughts, Carruthers."

"Eh?" Jasper blinked. "I believe a penny is the usual going rate."

Candy tugged the end of his moustache, looking like a smug walrus. "I'd put a premium on yours. You're a deuced hard chap to unravel, you know. How long would you say we've known each other?"

Jasper frowned. Candy had been resident at the boarding house almost as long as he had. "Why, it would be years."

"A decade to the week." Candy shook his finger at him. "And yet, I could not tell you the first thing about what goes on inside your head."

A jolly good thing, too. "I don't imagine my thoughts are

anything out of the ordinary." Just the usual musings of a man with an invisible cat to return home.

Candy shook his head. "You're a puzzle. You take pride in your work. Your uniform is immaculate and the hours you keep says volumes about your devotion to the postal service. I'd say you're as particular about your work as you are about your dress."

Jasper blinked. Was Candy examining him as if he were lost mail? "I beg your pardon."

"But you're not merely a professional man, either. The attention you pay to people. Like the butcher's lad, what's his name? Colin." Candy nodded. "You care enough about him to remember he has a girl. Which only adds to the mystery."

Jasper's heart plummeted. "Mystery?"

Candy grimaced. "A figure of speech. When you're a man of leisure, you need to fill in your day. I amuse myself by playing detective."

"And you've fixed on me as the subject of your investigations?"

"I can't figure it out, you see. You're a pleasant chap. Never seen you argue with anyone. You have orderly habits and you work hard. So what is a man like you doing alone?"

Jasper swallowed. Not the interrogation he feared, but neither was this comfortable. "And have you solved the mystery?"

Candy frowned, stroking his chin. "A catch like you would not remain on the shelf long. Married to a childhood sweetheart and widowed. You're still grieving."

What would Patience think of this conversation? "I hate to disappoint. Married, yes, but my wife is very much alive and well."

"Estranged?" Candy stared at him. "I can't believe it. You're the most amiable man I know. Never heard you say a bad thing about anyone."

Jasper's mouth twisted. "I prefer to leave them as bad thoughts."

Candy shook his head. "Not healthy that. You should let it out. Vent."

"I disagree. It's not healthy to give in to anger. It gives it strength, creates a habit." Jasper's fingers tightened around his glass as he struggled to find the words he sought. "Like a trail created over time by many feet on grass. One pair of boots makes little difference, but when those boots travel the same path day after day, they leave an impression in the grass. At length, a trail appears, attracting more feet. The more one indulges one's anger, the less able one is to master it. Until you wind up with cases like that Burr child."

Candy rubbed a hand across his chin. "Denial's not the only way of mastering it, though. Channel it into something productive. I used to chop wood in my younger days. Still could."

Jasper raised an eyebrow. How many gentlemen of leisure chopped wood? "Not much opportunity for chopping firewood in London."

"No, but you see my point. In the military, we learnt to channel our rage into drills until, no matter what the circumstances, our commanders knew they could count on us to obey orders and act as soldiers should. Though I don't deny that during engagements it was hard to keep a level head—especially if a comrade was injured. Or worse... Hum." Candy frowned. "All right. So, you may have something there, but even so, the Burr case is an anomaly. How many murderers do you know?"

"Just the two."

Candy choked, his eye bulging so much it almost resembled his glass one. "What?"

He must be drunk. How strong was this whiskey? Jasper stared into his glass. "I don't like to discuss the matter, but my parents' marriage was very unhappy. They argued incessantly. One night, during an altercation, my father picked up the nearest object at hand—which happened to be a poker—and struck my mother. She died the next day, and my father sentenced to ten years' imprisonment. He died in jail. I was adopted by an uncle." Candy goggled at him. "Hope you don't believe that murder is hereditary."

"You don't—you can't imagine you're in any danger of repeating your father's actions?" Candy sounded choked. "Why—the very idea is absurd!"

"I do not want to put it to the test. I make it my practice to avoid any disagreement and where at all possible aim to make harmony my priority." Jasper downed the last of his drink and stood, placing the empty glass on the incidental table between them. "On that note, should you change your mind about wanting to share a room with me, I quite understand."

Candy shook his head, rising to his feet. "Good heavens, no. I—I thank you for what you've told me, Carruthers, and I assure you, it has not changed my opinion of you at all." He squeezed Jasper's hand. "I won't repeat what you've told me tonight, I assure you. You won't regret trusting me."

Strangely enough, Jasper didn't.

9

With no further sightings of the toad-faced man, the investigation into the stolen crate stalled. Jasper got an answer to the letters he'd left with the harbour master: the boat from Egypt did not report any strange happenings. The second boat from America apologised for being unable to answer his question: the crew members on the voyage in question had quit.

Giving up wasn't an option for Jasper. Nigel had not interviewed him again, but he'd had all the record books from the previous five years taken up to his office. He appeared to be looking into the operations of the Dead Letter Office with a fine-toothed comb. Jasper comforted himself by reflecting on the quality of his work and concentrated on dealing with the parcels of the day. It would be a few days before he could take the next steps in his investigation into the cat's origins.

Jasper paused before the mighty columns of the British Museum. The grey stone pillars, very similar to those supporting the edifice of the postal service building, contained the relics of civilisations past. A monument to human achievement.

Then again, were the relics the post office not also a monument to the civilisation of the present? The hopes, dreams, fears, and sorrows of a nation committed to paper and ink and trusted to the vast machinery of the postal service for their delivery—a monument any nation could be proud of.

Jasper shook his head. "Getting sentimental in my old age." He drew out the notebook in which he'd copied down the hieroglyphics from the cat's casket from his jacket pocket and climbed the steps.

There was quite a crowd in the foyer. Jasper circumnavigated a crowd of school children and turned left. He bypassed the grand staircase in favour of the Graeco-Roman gallery. The Greeks and Romans were not so distant from the Egyptians. It made sense to suppose the Egyptian collection wouldn't be so far off.

His hunch was correct. Jasper turned a corner and sarcophagi and sphinx replaced the marbles and satyrs. He meandered through the Egyptian galleries, finding a bronze statue of a cat. A dark patina had formed as the statue aged so it now appeared black, the statue lightened by gold ornaments in the cat's ears, a nose ring, and a decorative collar.

The cat's label proclaimed it to be a representation of the goddess Bastet, taken from a temple and dating from the late period. Such statues could be an offering to the goddess or an object for worship. A translation of the hieroglyphics on the base of the cat indicated this was an offering.

Jasper peered at the hieroglyphs, comparing them to the notebook he carried. This was beyond the skills of a casual visitor. He would need expert help to decode the text.

"And here we have one of our most famous pieces—the colossal bust of Ramses II. I think you'll all agree that colossal as it may be, a bust it is not. Ha!" The explosive laugh rattled throughout the gallery.

Jasper jumped. Confound it! Was he never to be free of Candy? He ducked into a corner.

"This beauty became part of our collection in 1840. It's part of a statue, the rest of which is missing." Candy held forth with his usual confidence. "Note the high standard of workmanship. Ramses was highly regarded by his people—or at least, highly regarded by himself. Hard to imagine our queen erecting a giant statue to herself, eh?"

What did he mean—our collection? Jasper sidled around the corner of a case so he could peer at Candy and his companions without being observed.

Candy stood at the centre of an attentive family group. A short, moustached father watched his two daughters and son with an indulgent air, while his wife and a grandmother stood at a short distance, much taken by a display of jewellery. A grandfather leaned on his walking stick, eying the statue.

"Looks somewhat unfinished, doesn't it? Where's the nose?"

"The nose is lost. But it's interesting that you noted the rough patches, sir." Candy ducked his head. "Our curators believe the craftsmen deliberately left the band on his forehead and his eyebrows unpolished, to make it easier to apply paint. Yes, ladies." Candy grinned at the two girls. "Applying paint is not necessarily a feminine art! Ha."

The two girls blushed and dimpled, and the group murmured approval.

Jasper watched. That use of 'sir' showed that Candy did not know the group. He wore a navy coat with a trim, and brass buttons, something in the manner of a doorman. Jasper had seen an identical uniform on the man who had stood at the entrance, counting the number of school children.

What on earth was he playing at? This was the time of day that Candy retired to his club. Or—Jasper narrowed his eyes—was the club an invention?

Candy expounded on Egyptian antiquities with the air of someone who knew what he talked about. "The statue depicts Ramses wearing the double crown, showing dominion over the upper and lower kingdoms. The statue was found in the Temple of Khnum, Aswan. It's hot, desert country along the upper reaches of the Nile."

"You've been there?" asked the group's patriarch.

Candy nodded. "In my military days we had a training camp in Egypt. On my days off, I travelled up and down the Nile in a hired boat. I tell you, the Thames has nothing on the Nile in terms of business. You couldn't swing a cat without hitting another boat on the Nile—or a crocodile. Beastly creatures. Not that you'd want to swing a cat in Egypt. Sacred animals regarded as the emissaries of the goddess Bastet."

Jasper shook his head. Trust Candy to bring his military service into the explanation!

"When are we going to see the mummies?" the boy piped up.

"That's the next stop. Follow me." Candy threaded his way through the exhibits with confidence. "Before we view the mummy collection, I want to draw your attention to the scroll here." With a flourish worthy of a showman, he indicated to a papyrus scroll. "You see before you an extract from the *Book of the Dead*. Care to hazard a guess at what the book contained, sir?"

The father peered at the scroll. "Instructions for preparing the body?"

"A good guess, but no. The *Book of the Dead* contained spells to help the deceased navigate the afterlife. You see here the scene of judgement, with the heart of the deceased being weighed against a feather. If his heart weighs more than the feather, it is promptly devoured. This being the case, there was a lot of interest in spells to make the, ah, transition to the afterlife, easier. Ha!"

As Candy led the way to the mummies, Jasper drifted after the group. He cleared his throat, attracting the wife's attention. "Forgive me, but I couldn't help overhearing some of the very interesting talk that man was giving. Is he your guide?"

She nodded. "You can hire them at the entrance desk. Most reasonable, especially when you consider the size of our group and the sheer number of exhibits. We would be lost without Captain Candy."

"Indeed," Jasper murmured. "I must avail myself of his services some time." He permitted himself a smirk. Candy might know about the cat, but now that Jasper knew his secret, the boot was on the other foot.

"And here we are—the mummies." Candy ushered his charges into a dimly lit room. "The Egyptians took a lot of care to preserve their remains for the afterlife. Their narrow tombs, sealed against grave robbers, contributed to their state of preservation, as did the mummification process itself. Inside the tomb, they provided the mummy with everything they needed for the afterlife. Food, drink, their internal organs—stored in special jars."

One of the young ladies shuddered. "Ghastly."

"No more barbaric than some of our customs," Candy told her. "To a Muslim, for instance, our custom of allowing the deceased to lie in state for many days is most abhorrent. Their tradition is to bury their dead before the sun sets on the day of their decease."

As the family dispersed to gaze at the mummies, Jasper sidled closer to Candy. "Are you an expert on mummies?"

Candy jumped. His mouth dropped open, his dismay only too clearly broadcast. "Carruthers! What on earth are you doing here?"

"More to the point, what are *you* doing here?" Jasper eyed Candy's uniform. "I understood that you spent your days at your club."

Candy's ruddy cheeks stood out in red relief against his skin—now as drained of colour as the marble statues of the Greek and Roman galleries. "I—well, I—" He gripped Jasper's hand. "You can't speak a word of this to anyone. Please, Carruthers." He glanced at the clock in the gallery. "We close in half an hour. There's a coffee shop around the corner—Baileys. I'll meet you there."

Candy had never seemed so eager to get rid of him. Something pulled at Jasper. Something unknown, but not altogether pleasant. "I'll see you there."

Had Candy pulled a fast one on him? Jasper looked from his bitter cup of coffee to the coffee shop, grimy windows casting a dim light over the crowded tables. Why chose to discuss a sensitive matter in a coffee shop with barely enough elbow room to lift one's cup when they lived together? Or was Candy that eager to resolve that matter?

A few minutes after five, Candy dropped into the seat opposite Jasper, attired in his usual suit. His red face and heavy breathing indicated he'd made considerable haste to get there. "Carruthers. Thanks for waiting."

"I am agog to hear your explanation. How long have you been leading this…" Jasper hesitated, "this double-life?"

Candy signalled the waitress. She didn't ask for his order but went immediately to the kitchen. "I got the job at the museum before I moved into the boarding house. That's why I took the room—it's close enough to the museum that I can arrive early enough to change into my uniform on the premises."

That explained why he'd never seen Candy in his work attire. "And your reason for taking the job?"

Candy winced. "The military pension doesn't go as far as

it used to, and, well, there's not much call for an old duffer like me who was only ever good at the one thing. I had to make ends meet somehow. Guide, well, it's not the most respected of jobs, but it's honest work, and I meet interesting people. It keeps me fit."

Jasper frowned. He and Candy were of similar years and being on his feet all day sounded like nothing so much as hell on earth. "Your gout?"

Candy grimaced. "From time to time my joints play up. I need to rest my feet. I'm lucky, the curator in charge of the guides' division had a father who served in my regiment, so he's sympathetic and lets me take the time off."

Jasper frowned. Candy described a perilous existence, one that he'd had no inkling of. "And the reason for the elaborate deception?"

Candy avoided Jasper's eyes. "This will sound weak to a man like yourself, but, well—at school they regarded me as a bit of a dunce. I was no earthly good at sports, for all I liked them. In the army, I was much the same." He hunched in his seat. "I've let you think I am a gentleman. To tell the truth, I'm an innkeeper's son from Essex. My mother taught me how to cook, and I used to help her in the kitchen. It's the only thing I was good at."

Jasper blinked. "Goodness." He had not expected that. "So, your military experience…?"

"I was in the catering division. An army cook." Candy sunk lower in his chair. "It was hard work. Carrying our equipment, seeing that our supplies were fresh and not tampered with, dealing with servants and guides who weren't always on our side… And then feeding a regiment of hungry men three times a day, in all conditions. I fought a pitched battle against hungry British stomachs daily. And I had to deal with the enemy trying to kill me at the same time. It was hard work—but did I get respect for it?"

The waitress placed a cup of milky coffee before Candy,

sparing Jasper the necessity of replying. "Your coffee, Captain."

Candy nodded his thanks. "The men were all right. Quick to curse you if food was late or insufficient, but they were good lads on the whole. Knew we did our best for them. The officers—they were another story altogether. Gentlemen all, and they took pains to make sure you knew it. Too good to socialise with the likes of menials, always made sure you knew you were inferior. I'd never been ashamed of being Essex-born or how I talked 'till they made me conscious of it."

Candy sipped his coffee. "And then I returned to England a decorated veteran, and people I didn't know thanked me for my service, and boys saluted me in the streets...at least until I opened my mouth." Candy stared across the table at Jasper. "I don't know if someone who is the genuine goods can understand, Carruthers, what that meant to me. No one had ever thought I was important before. No one had ever given me respect. I couldn't lose it. So, I—I learnt to talk properly, and I got a better class of tailor, and a respectable address, and here we are."

"Here we are," Jasper repeated. All those years of being annoyed at Candy's pretensions, only to find out they were fabrications!

Candy stiffened. "So now you know, what do you plan to do about it?" His ears flamed pink. "I've got too much pride to beg."

Jasper recoiled at the thought. Any scene in public would be distasteful in the extreme. "That won't be necessary." He paused, removing his eyeglasses and polishing them. "Provided you say nothing about my cat, I see no reason I should mention your choice of employment. Every gentleman deserves to have a hobby. I imagine that being a guide has no end of interest."

Candy's good eye shone. He reached across the table,

gripping Jasper's hand. "You're a true gentleman, Carruthers. I can't tell you what this means."

"Perhaps the least said on that subject, the best." If a conceited Candy was intolerable, an effusive Candy was just plain wrong. Jasper removed his hand and replaced his glasses. "Are you something of an expert on Egyptology?"

"I know the museum collection like the back of my hand." Candy ventured a smile. "I picked up bits and pieces of the history on my travels—that's how I got the job."

"Can you read hieroglyphics?"

Candy shook his head. "I know a few symbols, but you'd need a curator for that. What are you after?"

Jasper hesitated. He'd got as far as he could alone. "I'm trying to translate this." He took out his notebook, showing Candy the line of hieroglyphics he'd copied from the casket.

Candy picked up the notebook. "This is beyond me, I'm afraid, but I'm sure one of the curators could oblige."

"Will they still be at work?"

Candy shook his head. "I shall ask them tomorrow."

One more days' delay wouldn't be any issue. "That should be fine. Much obliged, Captain."

"Least I can do." Candy frowned at the text. "What's this about? I can't imagine you'd have much call for hieroglyphics in your business."

Jasper shook his head. "You'd be surprised."

As they stood to leave, Candy seized his arm. "Don't look now, but there's a fellow staring at you. I didn't want to say anything, but the man's been watching you the better part of a quarter of an hour."

"Watching me?" It was with difficulty that Jasper stopped himself from turning to look. "Are you sure?"

"I've never seen him before," Candy said. "And it's you he's kept his eyes on." He affected interest in one of the paintings on the coffee shop wall. "There. The rather slimy looking chap in the tweed coat."

Using the glass of the painting as a guide, Jasper pretended to straighten his tie. He scanned the reflections of the coffee shop patrons until he spotted the man staring at him. The hair on the back of his neck rose. What was the toad-faced man doing in a coffee shop so close to the British Museum?

"Know the blighter?" Candy asked, his tone casual.

"We haven't been formally introduced, but I know him—as a man who supplied the post office with a false name, prevented delivery of a parcel to the rightful address, and is the only suspect in a burglary of post office property," Jasper replied, careful to keep his tone mild.

"What does he want with you?"

"I've no idea. Unless he is afraid that I've recognised him…" Jasper picked up his coat from the back of his chair, preparatory to leaving the restaurant.

The toad-faced man hurried towards the door.

"He's going to get away." Candy took a few steps after him. "I'll call a constable."

"No!" His own vehemence startled him. "No," he repeated, slowly. "He'll run if he thinks himself seen. We'll follow him ourselves—find out where he's hiding."

"Leave it to me." Candy pressed the coin to pay for his coffee into Jasper's hand. "I'm an old hand at this sort of thing." He made his way to the door, sauntering past the crowds with his usual self-importance.

Jasper didn't even think to protest until he was out of sight. "Old fool!" He paid for their coffee and hurried outside, but Candy and the toad-faced man were both long gone. "What does he imagine he'll accomplish?" Jasper had no alternative but to make his way back home, knowing that Candy would return to their shared rooms—if he were able.

Mrs Hollins shook her head as she surveyed the dinner dishes cooling on the table. "You're sure I can't clear these away for you, Mr Carruthers?"

"No, thank you. Not until Captain Candy returns." Jasper tugged at his tie. It was now hours past their usual dinner hour, and Candy was yet to return.

She gave him a doubtful look. "I'll be turning in soon. I'd be obliged if you gentlemen wouldn't mind carrying these dishes down to the kitchen yourselves when you're done."

Jasper breathed a sigh of relief as she bustled out of the room, but he still couldn't relax. Confound it—Candy should be back by now! Where on earth was he?

A paw patted his leg, and then the cat sprung into his lap. Jasper caught his breath and leaned back in his armchair, shutting his eyes.

The cat kneaded him. Within a few seconds, he heard her low rumbling purr.

Jasper stretched out a hand to pet her head. In his mind, the cat was a 'she.' Strange, that. Even stranger, that even though the cat was responsible for Candy's protracted absence, some of the anxiety Jasper felt over his non-appearance faded with every nudge of the cat's paws. "You're an awful pest of a creature. You don't even have the decency to be in any way ashamed of the trouble you've caused!"

The car purred, pressing against his hand.

At last, he heard a loud voice at the door, followed by a thunderous step on the stair. Jasper set the cat aside and stood just as the door swung open. "You're back at last."

Candy grinned at him. "I am—and with a story to tell, too."

Jasper exhaled. Candy was in a good mood. Nothing too dire could have happened. "You'll be famished. You can tell me all about it once we've dined."

Candy's eyes fell on the waiting dishes, and his grin increased. "A capital idea."

The meal was not at its best, lukewarm and dried out by successive bouts of heating in the oven, but Jasper did not notice, impatient to hear all that Candy had to tell him.

Candy ate heartily. "They say company is the best sauce, and I am inclined to agree. You didn't have to wait, Carruthers, but I'm jolly glad you did."

"After you had gone to so much effort on my behalf?" Jasper shook his head. "I only hope that you haven't overexerted yourself and will suffer tomorrow."

"Put that from your mind," Candy assured him. "An old soldier like me is used to forced marches—" He stopped, glancing at Jasper with a look that on any other man might have been shy. "I apologise. I've been keeping up the pretence for so long, it's become a habit."

Jasper snorted. "I don't doubt that being an army cook required equal—if not more—exertions to those of an ordinary soldier."

Candy gave a solitary nod and returned to his meal.

At last, Candy declared himself full, and the two drew their armchairs up to the fire, glasses of hot water and whiskey in front of them.

"I trailed the chap for many blocks. Several omnibuses passed us headed in the same direction, but he made no move to hail one. Evidently, he needs to watch his pennies—a conclusion confirmed by our destination: a pawnbroker."

Jasper raised his eyebrows. This did not bode well for the toad-faced man. "Go on."

"He went inside and asked to speak to the owner. I followed him in and lingered behind a shelf while they conversed. He offered the money he had on him in return for his pledge, promising to pay the rest later. The broker refused. The man grew desperate, saying that he was being hounded incessantly and returning the item was his only chance or relief. The broker refused to return the item until the man paid the amount owed in full. After some fruitless arguments, the man left."

Candy refreshed himself with a sip of his whiskey and water. "He lingered outside the shop for some minutes, his face a mask of misery. Finally, he came to a decision and trotted away. I left the shop and hurried after him, taking care to keep my distance, but I do not think he would have recognised me even if he'd seen me."

Jasper nodded. He could imagine the scene. The toad-faced man had been desperate when he'd visited the post office—desperate enough to resort to robbery. He must be even more desperate now.

"The man turned the corner and disappeared. By the time I rounded the corner, he had vanished. I was in a low neighbourhood. The sounds of off-key singing and raucous laughter emitting from many of the buildings led me to suppose that they contained bars, perhaps even gaming houses. I went inside three such establishments, ordering a beer and wandering around in the hopes of spotting our fellow. On my third attempt, I succeeded. He sat at a gambling table, playing cards with two hardened-looking vultures. I decided I'd seen enough and made my way back."

Candy coughed. "Not a terrible night's work, if I say so myself."

Typical Candy—he was so pleased with himself! And yet Jasper could not find it in him to be annoyed. "You've done much better than I could ever have hoped."

"I noted down the address of the pawnbroker and the gaming house," Candy continued, toying with the end of his moustache. "So you can pass that along to the police."

Jasper took the paper with misgivings. There was more than enough here to lay the matter to rest. The cat had been delivered to the Trent Street house addressed to Mr Leighton. A man resident at that address frequented a pawn shop and claimed to be hounded by some unknown force. He turned pale at the sight of the crate being restored to the house, and blanched at a cat's meow. Was it possible that the toad-faced man had taken something from the crate and pawned it, releasing the cat's spirit in the process?

Jasper scratched his chin. What reason could the man have for attempting to steal back the casket? Was he trying to rectify his past misdeeds by restoring the stolen property? If so, could Jasper turn him in? The chap seemed to have learned his lesson…

"Penny for your thoughts, Carruthers."

Jasper glanced up to see Candy's complacent gaze resting on him. "Have they declined in value so quickly?"

Candy choked. "No—not at all! I didn't think—"

How easy it was to fluster the chap! "I am not offended, I assure you. I was thinking of the man the parcel belongs to; P. Leighton. It's his property, therefore it should be his decision whether this goes to the police."

Candy raised his eyebrows. "The man's up to no good. He stole from your department!"

"It won't be my decision that condemns him."

Candy's gaze softened. "Because of your past?"

Jasper winced. "The police officers that attended my

mother's death were not what you could call sympathetic. In my dealings with them in later life, I have found them inclined to hasty judgements that they are slow to depart from. I suspect that we do not know all the circumstances in the case. Therefore, it would be premature of us to involve the law—particularly as it is the right of the parcel's owner to decide if prosecution should take place, not us."

Candy heaved himself to his feet. "Agree to disagree. A run-in with the police might show this chap he's committed a serious offence and prompt him to make a clean breast of it. But let's sleep on it. You may feel differently in the morning." Candy muffled a yawn. "I'll sleep well, that's for sure!"

Jasper bid him a good night and drank the last of his whiskey. The decision was easy for Candy—*he* did not know about the cat!

Jasper's eyes widened. *The cat!* He'd had her in the sitting room while he waited for Candy to return. Where was she now? He scanned the chairs and sofa of their shared sitting room. But he could not see any telltale impressions of the cat's body.

Jasper returned to his room, patting the bed and the floor.

No trace of her. It was already much later than he usually retired. Nothing for it but to go to bed, trusting the cat would return in the night. He left his door ajar and changed into his bedclothes, listening out for the cat's steady purr. He was still listening for it as he fell asleep.

Nigel folded his hands together, looking across his desk at Jasper. "Why was I not informed of the theft of an item from the Dead Letter Office?"

"I apologise," Jasper murmured. "Since the night-watchman informed the police of the matter, I had also assumed that he'd filed the reports." In fact, Jasper had spoken to him the next day and confirmed that he had.

Nigel narrowed his eyes. "Very lax behaviour. The post should be inviolate. Any theft is a matter of great concern to the entire post office, striking, as it does, at the integrity and reputation of our service."

Now that was below the belt! "My department foiled a previous attempt to steal the package in question. In the course of my efforts to unite the parcel with its rightful owner, I spoke to the driver responsible for deliveries to Trent Street, who furnished me with a description of the man who refused delivery. When a man identical to that description attempted to claim the package, I had Miss Conway fetch the driver who identified him."

"What?" Nigel stared at him. "The same man who first

refused delivery of the package is the man you suspect of the crime? That makes little sense."

"Not on the surface," Jasper allowed. "There is more to this situation than meets the eye. I am continuing to look into the matter, Postmaster."

Nigel regarded him, his expression hard. His jaw tightened. For a moment, he looked very like his grandfather. "Have you visited the Trent Street residence in question?"

Jasper swallowed, resisting the urge to tug at his collar. He pressed his palms flat against his trouser legs in an effort to keep himself still. "No, I have not."

"It strikes me as the obvious point of enquiry."

Jasper licked his lips. "I would prefer to have all the facts in hand before entering upon a course of action that might prove…inflammatory."

Nigel slammed a hand down on his desk, the violence of the action rippling throughout the office. "You're prevaricating. This reluctance to take a necessary step in this investigation amounts to a gross dereliction of duty—or is this a confession that you are unfit to hold your current position?"

Jasper winced. Nigel had him where he wanted. "Not at all, Postmaster. I shall call on 14 Trent Street without delay."

Trent Street was in one of the better residential neighbourhoods of London, near enough to the city for convenience but distant enough to avoid the noise, bustle, and excitement of its less-refined citizens. Number 14 was much like its neighbours: presenting a smart appearance to the world, even as its closed curtains gave no hint of its owners.

Jasper rang the doorbell. He was not surprised when no answer was forthcoming. No one had swept the doorstep in a few days, and the flowers in the window boxes had a limp, neglected look to them. No doubt the London residence of some country squire—perhaps the holder of Foxwood Court? Maybe he'd left the city for the comparative charms of the country, and the skeleton staff remaining behind were only giving the housekeeping the bare minimum required to keep up the house in his absence.

His knock at the back door also went unanswered.

Jasper stood at the door, stroking his beard. Where to go from here?

A window on the house next door shot open and a carpet heaved over the windowsill. A reed carpet beater followed, proceeding to raise such a storm of dust that Jasper took cover. He ducked into the next garden and knocked at the backdoor.

The carpet was heaved aside, and a woman leaned out. "We're not buying anything," she said. "Nor making any donations, no matter how charitable."

Jasper bowed. "I'm making enquiries about the residents of the house next door and hoping you can help. There doesn't seem to be anyone home."

She studied him. "One moment." She shut the windows. Before long, Jasper heard her steps on the other side of the door. She ushered him into the kitchen. "You're a postman, aren't you?" She eyed his uniform. "What is it you want to know?"

"We're trying to ascertain the ownership of a parcel possibly delivered in error to number 14," Jasper explained. "For that reason, I'd be very interested in everything you can tell me about your neighbours."

The woman waved him towards a chair. "I'll do my best to oblige, but I'm not sure how much good it will do you. Lord Cross is in the countryside, and the rest of the household with him."

"Foxwood Court?" Jasper asked.

"That's right."

He permitted himself a smirk. So, he'd been right all

along! "Do you know much about the household that Lord Cross keeps?"

"Only what you'd notice from being neighbours. We don't have a lot to do with number 14—our mistress doesn't approve of the household, so we hold ourselves apart."

Now, this was interesting. "She doesn't approve of them?"

The housekeeper shook her head. It seemed she was enjoying the chance to put aside her work in favour of a gossip. "It's a bachelor establishment, and you know what they say about bachelors."

Jasper raised his eyebrows. "No?"

"Without the tempering influence of a lady, a gentleman's habits are bound to lead him to excess." The housekeeper pursed her lips in disapproval. "It wouldn't surprise me if there was smoking, drinking, and gambling to all hours. Lord Cross—even if he is a Lord—has a very nasty temper, and that speaks to some over-indulgence, doesn't it?"

"I suppose so."

"And that Mr Leighton, Lord Cross's secretary, published a very peculiar book. My mistress says she's not at all sure it's proper, and she wrote to the newspaper to complain."

Jasper blinked. "This Mr Leighton, does he still reside with Lord Cross?"

"As far as I'm aware. He was in London with him when he last visited, I can tell you that much."

Jasper scratched his chin. "A shortish man with an enormous nose and a remarkable resemblance to a dead fish?"

She shook her head. "Why, no. You're thinking of Mr Angel."

Now, this was *very* interesting. "A guest of Lord Cross?"

"Hardly! Not that he doesn't give himself airs enough. No, he'd have you believe that he's on the same level as a butler, though he is nothing more than a caretaker. He's responsible for the house when Lord Cross is in the countryside." The woman glanced towards number 14 and leaned forward, adopting a quieter tone. "He's been acting oddly these last few weeks. I've seen lights on in the windows at all hours of the night, and once or twice seen him glancing over his shoulder as he walks down the street. Just like a man with something to hide."

"And does he have something to hide?" Jasper asked.

"I'd say he's not my idea of an excellent housekeeper, but he must do a good enough job because Lord Cross seems satisfied with him. Though what use a man who faints at the sound of a cat is, I don't know." She nodded towards a tabby, dozing before the fire. "Ginger was shut outside one night and meowed to let me know. Angel's face! You'd think he'd heard a gunshot, he was that pale." She made a disapproving sound.

Jasper hummed. Things were starting to line up. "Thank you for all you've told me."

"You're most welcome. Now, if you don't mind, I best be getting back to those carpets."

Jasper made his way back to the post office. What he'd learned from the housekeeper backed up his theory: Angel had removed something from P. Leighton's crate and now believed himself haunted by it. His attempted theft showed an effort to put things right, perhaps—or was he a desperate man, doing everything he could to stave off destruction? The fact that he'd ended his night in a gaming house did not bode well...

Either way, he had more than enough proof now to either go to Nigel or confront Angel himself, but still, Jasper hesitated. He would sleep on it, he decided. The matter might seem clearer in the morning.

He stepped into the shared sitting room, still preoccupied with the matter. Almost at once, a warm body pressed against his ankles.

"There you are." Jasper stooped, reaching down to pet the cat. "I was getting worried about you."

The cat's rumbling purr answered him. Had she missed him, too? On an impulse, Jasper scooped her up. She did not seem to mind, pressing her head against his chin. Jasper felt her purr vibrate through her body. "Good cat."

A choking sound alerted him to the fact that he was not alone. Candy stared at him from an armchair, his face a glassy white.

Jasper froze, fingers tightening around the cat. "I—"

"So. I'm not going mad." Candy staggered to his feet. "It's really there? But—" He turned an anguished look on Jasper. "What is going on?"

Jasper looked down at his arms cradling thin air. Though they seemed empty, the cat's purr was very audible. "I'm not sure myself. I've got a theory—but, well. As yet incomplete."

"Ha!" Candy's laugh was a poor echo of its usual self. He staggered over to the drinks cabinet and poured himself a nip of scotch. "Suppose you tell me everything?"

Once again, Jasper realised he didn't have a choice.

For someone so loud, Candy listened with surprising attention. He did not interrupt Jasper once and made no comment even after he'd finished. For several long minutes, the only sound in their shared sitting room was the cat's contented purr.

Jasper laid a hand on the cat's back, feeling its warm body against the palm of his hand. He'd not felt this peaceful since before the fateful crate had returned to the Dead Letter Office. Incredible the difference having someone to talk to about the entire business made!

Candy fingered the end of his moustache. "What are you going to do now? Confront this Angel chap, or turn him in?"

"That's the problem." Jasper rubbed the cat under her chin. "Neither feels right."

"Still thinking of hunting for this P. Leighton and putting the case before him?"

Jasper nodded. "I can't help but feel there's more here than we know."

"You're putting an awful lot of weight on the fact the man tried to get the crate back. For all we know, he could have been intending to destroy it and hide all evidence of his crime."

Jasper sighed, letting his hand rest on his lap. "True. Still, if you'd have seen his absolute terror when he heard Bastet's meow, it would have moved you to pity. He was frightened out of his wits."

"Bastet?" Candy smirked at him. "I thought you weren't naming the cat."

Jasper started. When had he started thinking of the cat as Bastet? "It is rude to refer to her as 'the cat.' She is, in all probability, an animal of high rank and status."

"Ah, yes." Candy stood, coming to stand beside Jasper's chair. He reached down, patting Bastet. "I haven't spoken to the curator yet. I'll do that tomorrow." He paused. "Have you considered keeping her?"

So, Candy also assumed the cat was female? "I can't do that. She's the property of P. Leighton—whomever he is."

"Bastet is no ordinary cat," Candy protested. "It's unlikely that this Leighton fellow will appreciate her. For all we know, he's trying to get rid of her. Wasn't the crate returned to sender from Foxwood Court as well as from the London place?"

Jasper frowned. Bastet nudged his hand, and he stroked her again. "I agree that is not promising... But at this stage, we do not know enough to say that Mr Leighton won't care for her."

"How many chaps do you know who would accept an invisible cat?" Candy shook his head. "Perhaps I am asking the wrong fellow. *You* seem to have taken her in stride."

Jasper grimaced. "I was as much shaken as you were, I assure you. Only the fact that my job"—Jasper paused, not yet ready to reveal to Candy the perilous state of his employment—"that is to say, only my devotion to my job induced me to return to the Dead Letter Office the day after my discovery."

Candy chuckled. "You sell yourself short. You've got nerves of ice, Carruthers. I'm sure you do yourself a massive disservice."

Jasper smiled, his mind preoccupied with his near slip. He'd almost confessed to Candy in just what dire straits his career stood. He couldn't allow himself to confide thus in the captain. Candy would surely use the knowledge to his advantage.

He already knew that Jasper was concealing an invisible cat, removed from the post office without permission. Candy could destroy him at any moment.

Candy gave Bastet a final scratch. "I'm turning in. You've given me a lot to think about—but I have to say, I'm pleased you confided in me, Carruthers. If only so I know that I'm not out of my mind—or if I am that I'm in damn good company. Ha!"

Jasper snorted. "Goodnight, Captain. Sleep well."

Candy squeezed Jasper's hand in farewell then walked to his bedroom. Jasper could hear the sounds of his night-time preparations through the door.

It was well past the hour that Jasper should be in bed, and yet he found himself reluctant to move. His reluctance wasn't simply due to Bastet, curled up and cosy on his lap. No, Jasper's sense of relief was so profound and so welcome he had no wish to end it by moving. Not even the knowledge that he had a long day ahead of him tomorrow was enough to get him moving.

And that was a problem.

Jasper's brow contracted, his hand coming to a halt on Bastet's back. In Candy's company, he was taking risks—confiding in him truths he had told no one else and letting his guard down to the extent that Bastet had escaped, and Candy knew of her existence—and her invisibility. And now, he was delaying doing what he knew he should. Candy was a dire influence on him. Jasper's fingers tightened around the arm of his chair. He'd been so focused on Bastet and the toad-faced man, he'd left himself unprotected. The real danger here was Candy.

Candy raised an eyebrow as Jasper emerged from his bedroom wearing a black suit and tie. "Not going to work today?"

Jasper shook his head. "I have a prior appointment."

Candy's eye lingered on Jasper's black tie, but he made no comment. "I'm working the Egyptian galleries this morning. Should have ample chance to take your hieroglyphics to the curators."

"Splendid, thank you. I look forward to hearing the results."

At nine o'clock, Jasper set out for the train station, stopping to buy flowers on his way. A little after ten, he alighted in the small town of Havelock. It had not changed at all in the decades since he'd lived there, retaining its old-world charm even in the face of modernising influences such as the train station and the streetlights.

As Jasper stepped through the stone church gates, he felt as though he'd stepped back to his youth. The homely facade of St John's was as complacent as it had been throughout a lifetime of dull services and gentle homilies, as one vicar after another had fallen prey to the serene charms of the village.

Early honeysuckle bloomed, giving the fine morning a hint of spring to come. The church door stood open, inviting visitors to enter and reflect.

Jasper did not avail himself of the invitation. Instead, he followed the path around to the back of the church, where the graveyard sprawled like a neglected garden. A black-clad figure stood before a small grave. Patience.

Jasper took off his hat. Bowing his head, he stood beside his wife for several moments in silence, contemplating the monument.

~

Hope Carruthers
March 21st 1854
Let the little children come to me, and do not stop them; for it is to such as these that the Kingdom of Heaven belongs. Matthew 19:14.

~

"She would have been thirty-five years old today, if she had lived." Patience didn't look up from the gravestone. "She might be a wife, a mother, with children of her own; and us, grandparents."

Jasper never knew what to say. "I'm so sorry, my dear." It had been so long, he struggled now to picture now the tiny baby, pink and wrinkled and small—so very, very small. They'd all known from the moment of Patience's unexpected labour, that there was little chance of her survival, little chance even of Patience's survival. But it had still hurt. It had still left them stunned and reeling from the blow.

He knelt, placing his lilies alongside a small bunch of

violets—Patience's preferred flower. The headstone was cleaned of moss, and the surrounding grass trimmed. The warden kept it in good order.

At length, Patience sighed, turning away from the stone. Jasper put his hand on her back. "Shall we?"

They preferred to dine in town, at a restaurant close to the railway station. The service was not as good, but the anonymity—on this day of all days—was priceless. They ate in silence, preoccupied with their own thoughts.

As the server placed their coffee in front of them, Patience broke the silence. "Do you ever wonder what it would have been like if I had died and Hope had lived?"

Jasper winced. "Do not blame yourself. The doctors all agreed. There was nothing that could be done. A first pregnancy is always risky."

Patience continued as if she had not heard. "You would be free—a widower, with an adult daughter, no doubt established with a family of her own. Wouldn't that have been better?"

"But if you had died, there would have been no Nigel," Jasper reminded her. "To say nothing of the comfort your presence brings to so many." He squeezed her hand. "Put aside these maudlin thoughts. You are here, and I for one are glad of it."

Patience looked at him. "Glad—but you will not live with me?"

Jasper bowed his head. "I will not."

He braced for her questions, for her justified reproach. Instead, she picked up her coffee. "We mustn't delay too long. The hospital closes at five."

As he had so often on this anniversary, Jasper wondered at the sheer courage of his wife. How many women faced with such a loss would turn their private pain into a force for good?

They stopped by a florist's for fresh flowers before arriving at the hospital. The director waited to greet them, showing them over the Hope Ward himself. Patience stopped at every bedside to speak to the women and ask about their health and comfort, even conversing with the nurses on duty. Jasper watched from a corner of the ward, where he might be out of the way.

Patience never failed to put the women she spoke to at ease. Jasper noticed the gaze of the director resting on her, admiration in his eyes. There was plenty to admire: Patience was gracious, kind, charming, with the mark of quality that distinguished a true lady from mere good breeding. And yet, try as he might, he could find no feelings for her beyond his deep appreciation of her excellent qualities.

After the visit to the ward, their custom was to walk through the hospital garden. Between the wings of the hospital, space had been found for a fountain and a few rose bushes.

Patience fingered a leaf. "It's funny to think we've been visiting this hospital for years and never once have we seen these bushes in bloom."

Jasper studied her expression. "Do you want a divorce?"

Patience dropped her hand, turning to face him. Her eyes were the same clear blue-grey as the fountain water. "You've asked me that before."

"Not for many years." Jasper hesitated. "We can't go back to where we were before, but you should not have to live alone. If you ever met someone, I would not stand in your way."

Patience snorted. "A grey-haired divorcee. I'm a real catch."

"You must not have seen the way the director looked at you. He was taken by you, and I assure you, he would not be the only one."

Patience gave him a sharp look. "I'm not sure my husband should encourage such thoughts."

"Come, Patience. We both know I'm a poor husband." Jasper hesitated. "I would much prefer to be no husband and instead, a good friend."

Patience made no reply. She straightened her gloves and put her arm through Jasper's. "Let us go."

As they walked to the gates, a man stumbled out of the hospital ahead of them. From his dejected posture and the way he blinked in the afternoon air, not seeing any of the scene that lay ahead of him, it was clear he'd suffered a loss.

Patience stopped, instinctively allowing room for grief. "That poor man."

Jasper swallowed. He recognised the glassy gaze and the ill-fitting suit. Mr Angel stood before the hospital in an attitude of loss.

Angel shook himself and, like one in a daze turned, walked through the gates.

"Are you all right?" Patience asked. "Jasper?"

"I beg your pardon. I—I know that man."

Patience cast a startled glance after Angel, but he had already vanished into the stream of pedestrians passing the hospital. "Should we go after him?"

"No—I don't think he'd thank us for intruding on his grief." Jasper hesitated. "If you don't mind, I'd like a word with the hospital staff."

Recognising the Carruthers as respected guests of the hospital director, the nurse had no qualms answering Jasper's questions. "It's a sad case, that is. Abandoned by her sweetheart, as so many of our girls are. When he refused to marry her, her parents cast her out. It was through the support of her brother she came here."

The toad-faced man? "A devoted sibling?"

The nurse nodded. "He didn't blame her. He thought she

was as much sinned against as sinning, and it's my opinion he would have done everything he could to see her and the child safe and well. He paid for her place here. Only..." She sighed, shaking her head. "We did everything we could, but we couldn't save either of them."

"The poor man." Jasper thought of the dazed look on Angel's face. He couldn't have been more bereft if he'd lost a wife or child.

The nurse nodded. "Some would say this was a blessing in disguise, but when you see the grief left behind... No, a loss is a loss."

Patience put her hand on Jasper's arm. "Take me home."

They got a cab, a rare indulgence. Patience clasped his hand, sitting beside him. "You meant what you said, didn't you? If I had died, you would have mourned me the same way you mourn Hope."

"More, perhaps." Jasper placed his hand on hers. "We never knew Hope. You—I know precisely what I have lost."

Patience raised her head. "Have you lost me?"

Jasper had done his best to avoid this conversation. The four walls of the cab allowed no possibility of escape. He gripped the seat, trying to force himself into calm. "We were better friends before our marriage than after it. I respect you now as I ever did—but marriage is not built on respect alone, nor even friendship."

"No," Patience said. "Or at least, not for us. We both want more." She turned her measuring gaze on him. "Have you... met someone?"

He shook his head, finding his throat dry. "What makes you think that?"

"This is more direct than you've been in years—perhaps ever."

Jasper coughed. "Yes, well. You can't teach an old dog new tricks."

"We're neither of us that old." The carriage came to a halt outside the house. Patience and Jasper alighted, the subject dropped. All the same, as Jasper returned to his rooms, he found himself repeating her words in his mind. Was Patience right? Had something changed?

15

Candy was in an expansive mood. "I got the goods all right. The curator delivered and then some! He was very enthusiastic about our find. Wouldn't mind having a closer look at it, he said."

Jasper winced. "I hope you told him that was impossible?"

"Naturally, naturally. I won't give the game away." Candy paused, his face registering shock. He shut his eyes, forcing himself to lean back in his chair. "I'm never going to get used to this."

"Bastet?" Jasper asked. He got his answer as the cat's deep rumble spread throughout the room.

Candy stretched out a hand, caressing thin air. "How on earth you kept her a secret is beyond me. I was a gibbering mess! If you hadn't been there to reassure me that I was not imagining it…" His gaze rested on Jasper, a worshipful light in his eye. "You are a man in a million, Carruthers."

Patience's question popped into Jasper's mind. *Had he met someone?* He tugged at his collar. Nonsense—Candy was a room-mate and an unwelcome one at that. "And what did the curator tell you?"

Candy pulled Jasper's notepaper out of his jacket,

spreading it out in front of him. "The inscription identifies the casket as containing the remains of Aziza, beloved companion of Ameres, High Priest of Osiris, who, leaving this world before her master, he entrusts to the goddess Pakhet, hoping they will meet again in the afterlife."

"Aziza," Jasper repeated. "So, she has a name."

"It means precious—as she certainly is." Candy stuck out his forefinger, no doubt rubbing the cat under her chin. "Aren't you?"

It was disconcerting watching him interact with an invisible cat. Candy seemed to have gotten over his hesitations. He stroked Aziza with a fond, almost paternal air, displaying unexpected warmth.

Jasper caught himself. Unexpected warmth from a man as full of hot air as Candy? "So this Ameres chap. Is anything known about him?"

"Not an awful lot. He seems to have lived in the New Kingdom, roughly around 1200 BC. His name was on a few monuments, and his tomb was found—robbed, but a few paintings remained. Turns out he was very fond of cats."

"I could have told you that."

"Ha!" Candy barked. Then, he winced. "Steady on!" He lifted his hands as though placing something on the ground. "Sharp claws for a three-thousand-year-old cat."

"I daresay you surprised her." Jasper snapped his fingers. "Come on, Aziza." He felt foolish—how on earth would he know if she even looked at him?

The furry head that pressed against his hand told another story.

"She seems to know you're looking out for her." Candy watched with an air of satisfaction at odds with the situation.

"Knows where her food comes from, is all." Jasper put a saucer of milk down for her every time they shared a pot of tea, and he made sure that she had water and food before he left for the day. He let his hand rest against her back, feeling her sleek fur. A short-haired cat. In his mind, she was a lean, black-haired cat, although he had no idea if that was accurate. Any hairs Aziza left behind were also invisible. "Did the curator tell you anything more about her?"

"As a matter of fact, yes." Candy weighed his words. "Last year, some archaeologists uncovered a ruined temple dedicated to Pakhet, adjoining a burial ground containing thousands of mummified cats. The markets in Cairo were full of them, the better specimens making their way to museums and collectors, while the more decayed specimens were bought in bulk by fertiliser companies."

"I remember hearing something to that effect." Jasper scooped Aziza up. "That won't happen to you, will it, my precious?"

Aziza meowed. She wriggled in his arms, resettling herself. The rough rasping sound that followed indicated she was grooming herself.

"As particular about her coat as you are. Ha!" Candy slapped his leg, leering at Jasper. "You're a matched pair."

Jasper did not see any humour in Candy's remark. "Only until we find her true owner." He put her down on the floor. "Off with you."

She appeared disgruntled, leaning against his leg instead.

Candy lit his pipe. "There's something else. This is speculation, mind… But can I take a look at the casket?"

"By all means." Jasper fetched the bag he kept it in.

Candy lifted it out with care. He traced the stone carving of the collar. "Just like Johnson suspected." He tapped the hollow. "This incision would most likely have contained a precious stone."

So, Angel *had* removed something from the crate! "Any idea when it was taken?"

He shook his head. "Impossible to say. It could have occurred in Egypt, or, well, at any point, though if you ask me…"

Jasper stared at the case. "You suspect Angel."

"Think about it—the man is alone in the house. He gets a delivery. He opens it, sees the stone. Who is there to know? He returns the crate to the mail service marked 'not known at this address.' With the labels removed, he knows the box is going to become lost in the mail system and destroyed. No one would ever know—until you trace it back to him."

Candy nodded, pleased with his theory. "He panics, realising that you will not stop until you deliver the box. He tries to claim the package, and when that fails, he goes to the pawn store, thinking his only chance is to regain the stolen property before he is found out. In the interim, greed has got the better of him and he has spent the money he received from pawning the stone. In desperation, he goes to the only place he can think of to raise the money needed—the gambling table." Candy paused to take a puff of his pipe. He blew out a stream of smoke, beaming at Jasper. "What do you think of my theory?"

"Good—to a point. But you've left out Aziza." She pressed against Jasper's legs. "My supposition—going from the deteriorated condition of the letter and the dead mouse found in her crate—is that Aziza made the journey from Egypt to England dormant. She was delivered to Foxwood Court, returned to sender, and arrived at 14 Trent Street where something happened—"

"The removal of the stone," Candy interjected. "It all fits!"

"Something happened," Jasper repeated, "that caused our sleeping cat to wake. That something is connected to Angel, as is obvious from his reaction to the noise of the neighbour's cat and Aziza's meow in the post office."

"A guilty conscience. Or perhaps Aziza is haunting him until he returns her stone?"

"That doesn't explain why she's now here with us—unless she is bound to remain with her casket. Did the curator mention anything about that?"

Candy coughed. "I couldn't ask him if he had much experience with invisible felines. Or even ghost cats. I asked about making mummified animals, and what he thought about the theory that the ancient Egyptians practised sorcery and other arts since lost to mankind, but he couldn't tell me much. Got the impression he thought I was rather an old duffer."

Jasper winced. How many times had he used those exact words to describe Candy? "You did well. We're a little further ahead now. We know where she came from, at least, and we have a better idea of why she's here."

"But still no idea what to do about it." Candy frowned at his pipe. "Even if you're not a fan of the police, this Angel chap's no prize. Stealing from his employers, gambling, deception and robbery. The man's a wrong 'un, through and through."

Jasper stroked his chin. "But a devoted brother."

"What?"

He sighed. "I saw him today. At the St. Bridget Hospital for Woman in Need." Remembering the sheer hopelessness of Angel's posture made Jasper feel like every word he spoke was a betrayal. "His sister found herself in, uh, a delicate condition—and alone. He paid for her admittance to the hospital and, I infer, was preparing to care for mother and child afterwards, if all had gone well."

"Gracious." Candy frowned. "It did not go well?"

Jasper shook his head. "Neither mother nor child survived."

"I say. That puts a different perspective on things. What Angel did was wrong, but if it was to help a mother and child in need…"

Jasper rubbed his forehead. "My thoughts exactly. We must do something, but what, I do not know."

"We could keep Aziza." Candy blushed. "The post office

believes her stolen. Why don't we just take care of her? Let Angel look out for himself."

Jasper frowned. "Aziza is the property of P. Leighton and it is my job—no, my duty—to see her delivered to him. The difficulty is figuring out how to do that without landing Mr Angel or myself in trouble."

"Why would you be in trouble?" Candy demanded. "You've done nothing but seek her owner."

"I brought home her casket." Jasper nodded to it. "Removal of mail from the post office without prior permission is a fireable offence."

Candy looked at it. "Surely in the circumstances, no one would hold it against you. Why, you stopped it from being stolen!"

Jasper could think of one person who would hold it against him. "I'm afraid… I must go to bed. Long day tomorrow." There was always a lot of mail waiting for him when he returned from his day off, and no doubt he would be summonsed to see the postmaster. Nigel would want an update on the investigation.

"Don't think on this too long, Carruthers. That's my advice." Candy puffed away at his pipe. "That's your problem, you know. You think too much."

Jasper glanced his way. "If I'd rushed in and reported Angel before now, he might have been grieving his sister from a jail cell. I will not make a rash decision that I later regret."

"That may be so, but delay too long and the decision will be taken out of your hands." Candy took his pipe from his mouth, regarding Jasper. "Nothing ventured, nothing gained. Life's nothing without risk."

Jasper raised an eyebrow. "Are you saying I don't live?"

Candy choked. "Wouldn't dream of it! Apologies, Carruthers—spoke without thinking!"

Jasper smiled thinly. "Goodnight."

Jasper shifted, struggling to settle in his bed. The exchange troubled him, lingering despite Candy's denial. *Are you saying I don't live...?* The implied criticism stung. And yet... For all his diligence, he was no nearer to returning Aziza to her rightful owner. Was he simply being careful—or avoiding an unpleasant duty?

16

Nigel arrived in the midst of elevenses. He ignored Jasper's greeting, stared at the teapot and biscuits, and waited until all three staff members were standing before he spoke. "I have been looking into the operations of the Dead Letter Office since my appointment as postmaster of this office, and in that time, it has become apparent to me that this department direly needs an overhaul—an overhaul that you, Mr Carruthers, are ill-equipped to provide."

Jasper's mouth tasted sour. He knew that Nora and Baxter looked his way, but he kept his gaze fixed forward, on a spot beyond Nigel's shoulder. "I understand, Postmaster."

Nigel continued as if he hadn't heard. "This department needs strong leadership as it undergoes these changes. It needs an active, younger man, one who has the strength of character and determination to see them through—even though that might lead to disagreements. Mr Lea, you're a man with a reputation for bravery. I am promoting you to department head, effective immediately."

Baxter's eyes widened. "But, Mr Carruthers—" He glanced at Jasper. "I—I couldn't. I mean—this is so sudden."

Nigel's brow tightened. "If you do not accept the appointment, Mr Lea, I will find someone else to fill the vacancy."

Jasper could not allow Baxter to pass up such an opportunity. "There could be no one more suitable than you, Mr Lea. Don't make a hasty decision." Jasper turned to Nigel. "A decision this momentous should not be made on the fly. Can we allow Mr Lea some time to consider it?"

Nigel pursed his lips but nodded. "Give me your decision by the end of the week, Mr Lea. Mr Carruthers, I will see you in my office."

Father and son walked through the halls of the post office in silence. It would have been hard to converse anyway, the halls full of postmen wheeling trolleys of mailbags, or carrying the bags to and from the sorting offices.

Jasper swallowed. The first time Nigel had entered these corridors, it had been on his shoulders when he had been allowed to see his father's place of work as a special treat. Jasper shook his head at the recollection. Nigel had come a long way from that plump baby, clutching a biscuit in one hand and Jasper's hair in the other. He'd clung to his father for reassurance against the lines of strangers. Now... Jasper's mouth quirked, despite the situation. Nigel did not need reassurance from him or anyone else. He was a law unto himself.

Nigel waved Jasper into his office and shut the door behind him. He did not speak until he was seated at his desk. "I'm sure my decision was no surprise. You must have known that you were ill-suited to the role of department head for some time."

Jasper lowered his head. He'd been braced for this dismissal ever since his first interview with Nigel. "You've chosen well in Mr Lea. He has the vision and the determination to see the Dead Letter Office brought up-to-date with the rest of our postal service."

Nigel leaned back in his chair. "That only leaves the

problem of what to do with you." He picked up a letter opener, twirling it as he spoke. "Your presence will be a hindrance to Mr Lea as he reforms the department. The respect he seems to think he owes you—not to mention your out-dated ways—will impede the necessary changes. I suggest that you resign. It will be far more pleasant for you and the department."

Jasper tightened his hands into fists. He spoke carefully, making each word clear. "I must respectfully disagree with you, Postmaster. I have seen many changes in my career with the postal service, and I have not stood in the way of any of them. Ask my colleagues, they will tell you how affable I am. My presence in the department will not detract from Mr Lea's efforts in any way."

Nigel narrowed his eyes. "I'm giving you a chance to leave with your dignity and reputation intact. You can refuse it, but you'll be leaving anyway—in disgrace."

Jasper's throat tightened. Nigel meant every word he said. "Why are you doing this?"

Nigel sneered. "If you'd bothered to spend any time with your son, you wouldn't have to question his motives. You would *know*."

"I respected my son's wishes and allowed him his autonomy," Jasper replied. "You only had to say the word and I would have spent my entire Sunday with you."

"One day a week. What kind of father comes with visiting hours?"

Jasper pinched the bridge of his nose. He'd seen his father only two hours a week, and that only if the guards had deemed his father's behaviour good enough—not that his father was any glorious prize, muttering threats against the guards and anyone he thought responsible for his incarceration. Jasper spent the entire visits terrified.

"Is this a request for more of my company? Because I assure you, these extremes are unnecessary."

Nigel snorted. "No. I mean to make sure you regret choosing your career over your family by taking the latter away. I'll give you until the end of the day to consider my offer. Dismissed."

For once, Jasper didn't move. "I chose to give your mother her happiness rather than burden her with the presence of a husband she found wearisome. My career had nothing to do with it."

Nigel looked up. "The long hours you worked, unasked for. What was that if not the chance of scraping an advancement?"

"Ask my colleagues—not Mr Lea and Miss Conway, but those who have known me years. Ask them whom the least ambitious department head they know is. Ask them how many times I have declined promotion. No—you can accuse me of many things, Nigel, but ambition is not one of them."

His son scowled. "You're a department head, aren't you? Having reached the pinnacle of your ambition—small as it was—you've stayed put."

"Once I'd reached the salary necessary to support your mother and her establishment and keep myself I had no reason to aim at a higher rank." Jasper pursed his lips. "I wonder, have you considered the effect on your mother should I become unemployed? I will not be able to support her."

Nigel frowned. "She will live with me."

Jasper tutted. "Is that what she wants? Your mother has always prized her independence and I fancy that she will not enjoy relegating the position of the lady of the house to your intended."

"She will adore Maud," Nigel said. "And it is unfair to expect mother to do everything. She is no longer a young woman..." He trailed to a halt, studying his father with something new in his expression. "Our engagement is not official—her parents have not granted their permission. How did you…?"

Jasper removed his glasses. "I may have been an unsatisfactory father for many years, but you have been content to express your antipathy from a distance. This sudden outbreak of, well, hostilities must be predicated in something —and from the direction our conversations have taken, I fancied you might be contemplating yourself in the role of husband and father."

Nigel stood, leaning against his desk, his palms flat. "There you go—presuming to know me," he spat. "You have no right to speak to me as though you cared! You've always been selfish, pretending to put others first but only ever concerned with your own comfort and convenience."

Jasper replaced his glasses. "Are you punishing me for being a poor father, or for not being the father you wanted?"

Nigel stared at him. He set his jaw and walked to the window. "You have the choice to retire now with your dignity intact, or to persist in your selfishness and be unmasked as the cad you are."

Jasper's ears thundered, roaring with the fury of a storm. He shut his eyes. "I will trust in my reputation and the fairness of the postmaster general."

"Don't trust in Postmaster General Raikes too much." The window glass reflected Nigel's satisfied smirk. "I notified him of your absence yesterday. He—like me—was very unimpressed that you would take a day off when your department needs your presence. He agreed to you being stripped of your position."

Ah. So that was how Nigel had done it. "I have taken the twenty-first of March off every year since the year of my marriage," Jasper said. "Before you make too big an occasion of it, I would consult your mother and make sure she wishes the anniversary to become public knowledge."

The window showed Nigel's eyes widen, the flicker of

doubt interrupting his composure. It was gone quickly, replaced by a scowl. "Dismissed, Carruthers."

"Yes, Postmaster." Jasper bowed and walked out of the room.

His shaking legs carried him as far as the stairs. Jasper leaned on the bannister, taking in a deep breath and letting it out. The sting at being replaced by Baxter had been overshadowed by this greater fear—the fear of losing his position entirely. Nigel had every intention of making good on his threats. Would he succeed?

17

"No. You stay there." Getting out of the house without Nigel following him as a baby had been hard. Leaving their rooms without taking an invisible cat with them was even harder. Jasper squeezed out the door, hoping that Aziza was on the other side of it.

Candy stood in the hallway, already wearing his coat and hat. "It's as though she knows we're going somewhere special. Doesn't want to miss the fun. Ha!"

Jasper shook his head. "It's merely a trip to the country-side." Anyone would think from Candy's attitude that they were setting off on holiday.

As Jasper pulled on his coat, scarf, hat, and travelling gloves, Candy selected a stout walking stick from the umbrella stand and picked up the picnic basket Mrs Hollins had prepared for them. "After you."

He must still be sore from his summary demotion, as Candy's courtesy did not grate as it usually did. He waited for Candy on the steps, musing at how quickly his world could change on its axis. A few weeks ago, if anyone had told him he would be spending his day off in Candy's company, he would have laughed at them. And now... His gaze travelled up to the window of their shared rooms. Aziza had a lot to answer for.

"Off we go." Candy stomped down the road with zest. "Amazing what a difference even an hour can make, don't you think?"

Jasper nodded. He usually left for work two hours later when pedestrians and carts packed the streets. At this early hour, he and Candy were the only people about. "Being a Sunday makes a difference, too."

"Undoubtedly. But I always say that if you're going anywhere, you're best to make an early start."

Jasper half expected to hear 'in the army.' Instead, Candy whistled. He shook his head. A schoolboy on an outing could not have been in any better spirits than Candy now.

The party mood persisted until they were on the train and even after they'd alighted at Rotheram. Candy took a deep breath of the country air. "Taste that! Nothing like London, what?"

"Indeed." Even though it was still cold, flowers bloomed in window boxes and hanging baskets of the homely country station. The hedgerows were thick with leaves, and the grass a hearty green. "Why, we've seen more greenery this morning than we have the entire month in London."

The stationmaster stepped forward to collect their tickets. "And where might you two gentlemen be going?"

"Foxwood Court," Candy said. "You know the place?"

The stationmaster coughed. "There's not a person in these parts that doesn't know the court." He frowned, giving them a second look. "No one from the house indicated they were expecting visitors."

"Oh, we're not guests," Jasper interjected. "We're interested in seeing the house."

The stationmaster's eyes fell on Candy's picnic basket and his gaze cleared. "Sightseers. You'll be wondering how to get to the house. There's a local lad with a cart who would be happy to take you. Five pence is the going rate, there and back."

Without further ado, the lad was found, the cart paid for, and Candy, Jasper, and the picnic basket settled in the back.

Jasper lurched as the cart encountered a deep pothole. "We're in the country all right!"

"Steady." Candy settled a firm hand around Jasper's waist, holding him in place.

As the cart continued on a more even keel, Jasper breathed out. "You can release me now, Captain."

Candy did not remove his hand. "And where would the fun be in that?"

Jasper shot him a quizzical look. Candy's glass eye met his gaze blandly, but his remaining eye twinkled with mischief.

Jasper's chest gave a flutter he had not felt in many decades. Did Candy's excessive good humour have an explanation beyond the anticipation of a pleasant day in the countryside? If it did, the thought was not altogether abhorrent.

Jasper busied himself with his handkerchief, trying to keep his expression calm. "Tell us about the inhabitants of Foxwood Court. You said it is the ancestral home of Lord Cross?"

The lad nodded. "There's been Crosses in Foxwood as long as it's been Foxwood, or so my father says. The present lord, he's been lord since before I was born."

Jasper nodded, trying to ignore the fact that Candy's arm was still around him. "What sort of man is he? Pleasant?"

The boy laughed. "Lord Cross, pleasant? No—he takes after his name. Bad-tempered, exacting, doesn't suffer fools. A clever man, and he does the town proud, but pleasant? No, not on your life!"

Jasper's heart sank, thinking of Angel. "He is not what you'd call...a forgiving employer?"

The boy tilted his head, thinking about this. "Well, he is and he isn't. You can't say he's not fair, and he built the school all on his own behest. But he's strict. Awful strict, he is, and one for the rules."

"And Mr Leighton?" Prompted Candy.

"You're hoping to see the collection?" The boy shook his head. "I wouldn't, not even if you paid me to look at it! But I suppose you know best what you're about."

Candy and Jasper exchanged a frown. "I beg your pardon," Jasper said. "What collection are you referring to?"

"You don't know? Then forget I said anything." The boy grimaced. "Reckon it's by appointment, anyway. It's the galleries and the old parts of the house you want to see." The lad seemed keen to change the subject and kept up such a commentary on local surroundings that they did not have the chance to ask him anything further.

The horse plodded down a tree-lined drive, coming to a halt in front of a house that looked like it had come straight out of an engraving of stately homes of the ages. At least four different architectural styles were present in its many wings, arches, towers, and additions.

"Well!" Candy stroked his moustache, his gaze resting on the house. "This was worth making the trip for. What a magnificent house!"

"Hundreds of years old," said the boy, with local pride. "Visitors call at the back door."

Sightseers were the responsibility of the housekeeper, Mrs Rice, a crisp woman with an abrupt way of talking. She sized Candy and Jasper up in a matter of seconds. "Here to see the house?" She asked. "The family is at home, so you cannot see all of it, and we ask that you keep your noise to a minimum."

Jasper gave Candy a stern look. "We quite understand."

Mrs Rice took them through a formal dining room, pointing out antique furniture and architectural flourishes. The tour continued through a ballroom which contained noteworthy artwork, and the drawing room—clearly recently used by the house's owner. Jasper nodded in response to Mrs Rice's commentary on the fireplace, but his gaze rested on the bright red ball resting on one of the sofas. As Mrs Rice turned to lead them to the next point on their tour, he ventured a question. "Is Lord Cross fond of animals?"

Mrs Rice led the way up a grand staircase. "Fond? He doesn't dislike them, but he's not what I would call an animal lover. He is too concerned with his business affairs and the management of his estate. Lord Cross has a wide correspondence." She spoke of her master with respect, but Jasper thought he detected a note of pride.

"No pets, then?" Candy asked.

Mrs Rice considered. "There are the kitchen cats. A house this side must have a cat or two to keep the mice down, but they rarely come into the family's part of the house."

Jasper scratched his beard. That boded well. "Any dogs?"

"The lodge-keeper, Brown, he keeps a pack of dogs for hunting, but Lord Cross isn't what you'd call a committed sportsman. He keeps up the tradition, as was his family custom, but he won't ride for the pleasure of it." She opened a door, stepping back to allow Candy and Jasper to enter. "The long gallery."

This was a star attraction: a long room running the length of the wing, with portraits of the Cross family at intervals. The Cross family were distinguished for stubbornness, intelligence, and fits of temper, explained Mrs Rice—many of them had met their ends in battle or duels.

"This chap looks a warlike fellow!" Candy peered at a great-grandfather of the current Lord. "Let's hope his descendant is an easier man to work with, what? Ha!"

Mrs Rice smiled and shook her head. "Our Lord Cross is not an easy master, but he at least has the self-awareness to know it. He works us hard, but he makes sure we're compensated well."

"Is he a forgiving sort of man?" Jasper asked.

She shook her head. "He is quick to anger, and his tongue! When he is riled, I do not like to see him angry, no sir! He is quick to take action, but equally quick, once the matter is settled, to make amends."

Jasper breathed out. Perhaps things would not be as bad for Angel after all—

"Except where Mr Leighton is concerned," Mrs Rice continued.

Jasper's heart sank. "Mr Leighton?" Or perhaps Mr Angel was doomed.

"And who is this Mr Leighton?" Candy demanded.

"Lord Cross's distant cousin and heir, currently acting in the role of his secretary," Mrs Rice explained. "It's a funny thing, but although Lord Cross is careless of wrongs done to himself, he is exceedingly protective of Mr Leighton. In fact, I should say there is no faster way to rile his lordship than to insult Mr Leighton."

"Lord Cross has a lot of family feeling," Candy observed. "He's not a married man?"

Mrs Rice shook her head. "We're a bachelor establishment—though we have hopes in Mr Leighton. He recently adopted a son, so he clearly has an interest in the family line."

"How old is this son?" Jasper asked. Was the child likely to tease Aziza?

There was a pause before the housekeeper replied. "Master Julian is eight years old."

"Is he kind to animals?" Jasper winced. What would she think of such a question?

Mrs Rice did not seem to think it strange. "You should see him with old Tibby. She is not a pretty animal, having lost an eye and her fur rather matted, but Master Julian will sit next to her for hours, petting her. While he likes animals, they do not seem to like him. Our kitchen cats hide whenever he comes into the kitchen. It's a great source of sorrow to him, the poor mite."

Jasper pursed his lips. This did not bode well for Aziza. The kitchen cats were a better judge of character than a fond housekeeper.

Mrs Rice handed them on to a footman for the tour of the garden. The man, introducing himself as John, showed them over the formal gardens, the site where a maze was being contemplated, and the lake where a marble statue of uncommon interest overlooked a pleasing vista of the English countryside.

Candy waxed rhapsodic over the view. "I feel years younger just looking at it! You country fellows don't know how lucky you are."

Jasper's enquiry over Lord Cross's temper produced an answer identical to that given by Mrs Rice. One thing was certain—Angel could expect no mercy once his employer discovered his wrongdoing.

"You are welcome to walk in the park," John said. "Many of our visitors find it a pleasant spot to picnic, though we ask that you do not leave any rubbish behind."

"Naturally," Candy agreed. "I say, I don't know if this is regulation or not, but we heard something of Mr Leighton's collection… There's no chance we could see it?"

John frowned. "It's by appointment only, but I will enquire if Mr Leighton is available." He left them waiting on the house steps.

"What are you doing?" Jasper asked. "We know everything we need to. Lord Cross is a stern man, the house has cats enough, and by the sounds of things, a boy who is none too gentle with them."

"It's Mr Leighton we're interested in," Candy shot back.

"You can tell a lot about a man by what he places value on. This collection should be most interesting."

"If we get to see it," Jasper shot back. "We're intruding enough as it is!"

Before Candy could respond, the footman had returned. "Mr Leighton would be delighted to show you his collection. This way, gentlemen."

Jasper straightened his tie, glancing at his reflection in a suit of armour to make sure he was presentable. This meeting would decide Aziza's future. He could not afford to make any mistake.

Mr Leighton waited for them at the library door. He was a slight man of middle years, and he shook hands with them with what felt like genuine pleasure. "It is always a treat for me to show off my little collection. There are so few who appreciate it. Do we share an interest in the supernatural?"

Jasper's mind went blank. "I—"

"We keep an open mind," Candy said. "Know just enough to be interested, but not enough to come to any firm conclusion."

Mr Leighton beamed at them. "Wise. That is the right attitude to take—to be willing and open to learning more. A very strange incident that neither science nor religion could explain sparked my interest. My collection is my attempt to learn more—though once I realised how broad the field was, I did not try to curtail my interest." He led the way into a large wood-panelled room, lined with bookshelves, display cases, and an ample amount of desks and armchairs. The room was well used—a tray of tea things was placed on one table, and a cat dozed before the fire.

"This is the piece that started my collection." Mr Leighton paused in front of a portrait. "Joseph Leighton who died in this house over a century ago."

Candy started. "Why, he looks like you!"

"You flatter me, Captain. I have aged. Joseph, poor fellow,

did not. His ghost was seen by the residents of Foxwood Court—including myself and Lord Cross—although he has not appeared for a decade now."

"Laid to rest?" Candy asked, with a certain stiffness in his voice.

Leighton nodded. "I trust he is at peace." He motioned to a bookshelf. "From what I have gathered from my research, no one is sure what happens to a spirit once they pass over. Even contact with spirits via mediums do not produce clear results. We are no closer to understanding what goes on beyond the veil than we were in Joseph's time."

Much as the housekeeper and footman had, Leighton gave the tour of his collection with the skill of long practice. He showed a certain pride when discussing the volumes of the occult he had collected but reserved his enthusiasm for a nightmarish relic.

"A genuine hand of glory, gentleman. Are you familiar with the tradition?" Leighton indicated a display case.

Candy stared at the object within. "The British Museum has a similar specimen, though ours is not on display. Too morbid for public consumption."

"Smart," Mr Leighton agreed. "I've noticed mine has a very unfortunate effect on some of my visitors." He coughed. "The British Museum… Are you a curator, sir?"

Candy shook his head, stiffening his shoulders. "Merely a guide. I conduct tours through the museum."

Jasper felt his chest swell. Candy had set aside his pride—and Jasper had never liked him better. "Captain Candy sells himself short. I've had the pleasure of listening to him talk, and he is not only knowledgeable but an excellent speaker."

"Is that so?" Mr Leighton looked at Candy with new appreciation. "I should be delighted to have you return as my guest and speak at our village hall. I am keen to further the education of our neighbourhood and have been organising talks on subjects of interest. Should you be interested,

Captain, I am sure that you could tell us much about the museum's collection that would be most entertaining."

Candy coughed. He seemed to fight a blush. "I should be delighted, though there are curators far more knowledgeable than myself…"

"Knowledge is one thing, the ability to communicate it meaningfully quite another. I imagine that as a guide you have had the chance to refine your explanations until you can tailor them to your audience."

Candy stroked his moustache, expanding somewhat. "I suppose there is something in that. I shall consider the matter."

"Please do," Mr Leighton said. "Is there an area on which you would care to speak?"

Candy glanced at Jasper. "My commentary on our Egyptian artefacts is always appreciated."

"Egypt!" Mr Leighton's eyes gleamed. "Tell me more. I confess, I have a special interest in the traditions of the Pharaohs. It is one of my great disappointments that my collection so far lacks anything Egyptian."

Jasper glanced around the room. He'd been wondering about that. There were books, paintings of haunted castles, and portraits of people reported to be ghosts. But apart from the few pieces of Māori jewellery and clubs depicting the gods and monsters of distant New Zealand, there were no pieces of historic interest.

"The British Museum has the fortune of being well repre-sented in that respect, thanks to generous behests by notable archaeologists and the efforts of the museum directors."

Mr Leighton's head bobbed in eager agreement. "I have visited the museum many times, and I am always taken by the scale of the collection. In particular, the mummies."

"Ha!" Candy's laugh did not ring true. "Yes, the mummies are a perennial favourite."

Leighton's gaze grew wistful. "It is my ambition to own a

mummy of my own, an ambition not likely to be fulfilled soon."

Jasper frowned. "And why is that?"

Mr Leighton sighed, leaning against the display case. "The staff here are wonderfully loyal and dedicated, but they are… short-sighted when it comes to certain things. Egyptian artefacts are among them. Should I attempt to bring a mummy into the house, the staff will, as one, tender their resignations. They have not been open to negotiation on the subject."

Candy coughed. "Dear me. That is a blow."

Leighton nodded. "I am sure that in time they will get used to the idea… and there is always the London residence, though it is not as well suited as Foxwood Court to house a collection."

Jasper's mind raced. If Mr Leighton's staff opposed him adding Egyptian relics to his collection, that might explain why the crate containing Aziza's casket was first returned to sender. He stepped forward, hoping to mask his confusion by feigning interest in the display case.

But the contents of the display case took all thoughts of Aziza from his mind. Jasper stared at a pale, shrivelled object, wrapped around a candle, looking for all the world like a—

"Hand." Jasper felt a beating in his ears, his blood thundering. "Good Lord, it's a hand."

A hand grasped his arm. "Take his other arm, if you don't mind, Captain." Mr Leighton said. "It seems Mr Carruthers needs some air."

The rushing in his head increased. Jasper staggered and found himself in a firm grip. "Take it easy, Carruthers. I've got you," Candy said.

Jasper shut his eyes and leaned into Candy. He didn't think about how strange it was, to be so supported by him. At that moment, it did not seem strange at all.

19

"I am so sorry," Jasper repeated. He sat on a stone bench in the garden, his gaze fixed on the gravel path before him. The bare branches of rose bushes swayed in the breeze on the edge of his vision, the crisp country air acting as a restorative. His cheeks glowed with cold, but he had no interest in stepping inside the house a second time. "I had no idea the sight would take me like that."

"No apologies needed," Mr Leighton assured him. "You're not the first, and I am sure you'll not be the last."

"You're looking much better," Candy assured him. "You'll be right in no time."

Jasper pressed his lips together, removing his spectacles and patting his pockets in search of his handkerchief. "I should be used to this by now. Last year, after the dreadful Whitechapel business, there was a spate of letters sent by people claiming to be Leather Apron. One letter made its way to our department. It contained a finger. I'm ashamed to say I fainted."

Candy proffered his handkerchief. "No shame whatsoever. The more shameful thing would be to have no reaction."

"A large number of our staff have refused to enter the library altogether since I gained that piece. I had rather a hard time convincing them to let me keep it at all." Leighton sighed. "I assure you, Mr Carruthers, that you are in good company."

Jasper forced himself to smile. His stomach still roiled, but he felt able to walk. "You are very kind, Mr Leighton, but we cannot trespass on your goodwill any longer. I'm sure you are very busy."

"You are not keeping me from anything important," Leighton assured them. "We spend so much time at Foxwood that I have all business connected to the estate in hand. Though, Lord Cross did mention wanting to dictate a letter. If you're sure I can be of no further service…" He paused with what seemed like hope.

Jasper shook his head. "We cannot impede on your duties. We're already indebted to you for showing us your most interesting collection."

Candy shook Mr Leighton's hand. "The next time you visit the British Museum, mention my name. There are a few items not exhibited to the public that I think you would enjoy seeing."

Mr Leighton's face glowed like a child's on Christmas Eve. "You don't say! I shall be sure to you up on that offer. Thank you, Captain Candy, Mr Carruthers, and please consider giving us a talk sometime."

Behind them on the terrace, a French door opened. A dark-haired, bearded man stepped out, looking just past what was politely called the prime years. "Leighton!" he bellowed. "Your company, please."

Leighton turned, bowing in the man's direction. "Lord Cross," he murmured. "It was a pleasure to meet you both. Write to me and furnish me with your particulars. It is always a pleasure to meet fellow seekers of truth, and I am eager to deepen our acquaintance." With another round of handshakes, bows, and thanks, he departed.

"Well," Candy said, once the glass door had closed on Leighton. "He's not at all what I expected."

"Very different from Lord Cross," Jasper agreed. "But it is Lord Cross who is in charge of the staff."

"Including Leighton." Candy stroked his moustache. "Are you feeling up to walking in the park? I'll fetch the picnic basket."

Jasper agreed. He was not sorry to put the house behind them.

Foxwood Park was a proper forest, the trees gnarled with mossy trunks. Twisting paths wound through tunnels of trees with a canopy of leaves so thick that the air had the cool feeling of walking through a chapel. The trees then opened into clearings in which bluebells swayed in the sun, or the bright flash of daffodils danced in the breeze.

In one such copse, Candy spied a sunny bank that he thought would make the perfect setting for a picnic. "Old dogs like us need a bit of comfort. We can't get up and down like those young bucks."

Jasper placed his handkerchief on the grass and levered himself down onto it. "This is a charming view. I don't think you could have chosen better."

Candy cleared his throat. "The view is greatly enhanced by my present company."

What was he playing at? Jasper shot him a glance, but Candy was busy digging through the picnic basket. "It is not chilled, but I hope I can persuade you to join me in a glass of champagne, Carruthers?"

"Good heavens! Mrs Hollins didn't supply that."

Candy tugged at his moustache. "My little fancy. I hope you don't mind?"

"No—of course not. But the expense—"

He shook his head, waggling his finger at Jasper. "I won't

hear another word about the expense. I'm an old bachelor, I don't have anyone but myself to worry about. Your friendship means a lot to me, Carruthers, and if I want to give you a treat, I see no reason I shouldn't."

Jasper's stomach rolled with unease, even as his chest filled with warmth. "If you're sure, Captain, then I am very much indebted."

"Rudyard," Carruthers said, fussing with the cork of the champagne bottle and avoiding Jasper's gaze. "Rudy to my friends—if you're so inclined."

Jasper swallowed. "Rudy," he whispered, his heart pounding. "I'm Jasper."

Candy gave him a brilliant grin. Jasper found his gaze too much, removing his clean spectacles and polishing them once more. Utter nonsense! Why should his heart be threatening to burst out of his chest from the mere fact that Candy had shared with him his nickname? What on earth was he doing, giving Candy his own name in return? It would be impossible now to insist on keeping his distance…

Below it all, fear coiled like a snake. He could not trust this feeling. He could not let the moment sweep him up, putting himself even further in the power of a man with little tact and no self-awareness to speak of. Candy was a joke! Jasper's self-respect was at stake—as was his career! His job at the post office now depended entirely on discretion—and Candy was not discrete by any stretch of the imagination.

Jasper watched him struggle with the champagne bottle, vowing that he would be polite, and no more. He must put a stop to this before he did something he would regret.

"There." Candy divested the bottle of its cork and poured two delicate glasses of champagne. "To friendship."

Jasper clinked his glass to Candy's, his mouth tasting sour. "To friendship." The champagne was very welcome, washing away the taste of deception. Jasper sipped his glass, while Candy unpacked the basket. "Mrs Hollins has outdone herself! Look at this—a proper pigeon pie."

Jasper cocked an eyebrow. Mrs Hollins was a very capable manager, but to make their weekly food allowance stretch to pigeon pie was something else. "How much of the menu did you assist with?"

"Tsk, Carruthers—Jasper." Candy's ears were a fiery red. "I said not another word about the expense."

How many years had it been since anyone besides Patience had used his name? Jasper felt a warm glow overtake him. The champagne was potent! He must be careful not to indulge. "If you insist. But it feels wrong to share your bounty and not thank you."

Candy reached for Jasper's hand, squeezing it. "This is my thank you to you. Having someone to share my rooms with, who knows about my job at the museum and still treats me like a gentleman..." He coughed, turning back to the food. "This is but a small return of the pleasure your company has given me—and an expression of my hope that this is but the start of a very special friendship."

Jasper felt his cheeks heat. How on earth did one reply to such a statement?

"I don't know how I feel about Aziza living here," Candy said. "The park is pleasant, but the housekeeper did mention hounds."

Jasper took the conversational opening as though it were a life preserver. "I am more concerned about the boy. Children are not always gentle where animals are concerned."

Candy snorted. "Little devils. No, I'm inclined to think we would not be doing her any favours by bringing her here."

"Though, Mr Leighton is her rightful owner." Jasper worried his lip. Was he reluctant to entrust Aziza to a man who would view her as part of his collection—or did he not want to part with her at all?

"Here." Candy had cut thick slices of the pigeon pie. He

regaled Jasper with stories from his time both as an army cook and as a guide.

Jasper, against his better judgement, accepted a second glass of champagne. He found himself telling Candy about his brief career as a special agent. "I was roundly considered the best at spotting discrepancies and identifying those in the service who ceded to temptation and broke the sanctity of Her Majesty's Mail service. However, while I never failed to identify my man, I never once succeeded in taking him. When the moment came to spring the trap and make the arrest, my nerve failed me. I have the singular honour of being considered the most promising special agent to have never made a successful catch."

Candy leaned back on the grass, watching him through half-closed eyes. At this angle, his glass eye was indistinguishable from his real one. "I am not surprised. I've never met anyone as kind as you."

"*Pshaw.*" Jasper polished his glasses for a third time.

Candy sat up, putting his hand over Jasper's. "I mean it. I don't think you appreciate just how rare you are—" His weathered fingers brushed Jasper's cheek. "Carruthers—that is, Jasper. You know I have nothing but pretensions to being a gentleman, and you still respect me. Is it possible that we could, perhaps, be… more than friends?"

A few weeks ago, this would have been Jasper's nightmare. A day ago, it would be a complete impossibility. Today…

It wasn't the champagne. Jasper tucked his glasses into his breast pocket. He placed his hand on Candy's cheek. The warmth he felt astonished him. Candy's skin was rough, weathered by age and the harsh conditions of army life, but his blood was as warm as any man's, evoking an answering warmth in Jasper.

If anyone walked in on them now, they would split their

sides laughing! He was an old man, and Candy, too—they had no business acting like courting youths!

Jasper shut his eyes, leaning in. Candy stiffened a moment with shock but melted almost at once, his arms sliding around Jasper with gentle care. The initial leathery brush of skin and moustache gave way to the soft pliability of mouth and lips. Jasper deepened the kiss, feeling a rush of giddiness. His heart soared, elation in his veins. He felt as though he were a lost letter at last returned to sender.

20

"We may have missed our train, but a successful expedition, if I say so myself." Candy strolled down the road towards their shared apartment with a self-congratulatory air. "We should do this more often, what?"

Jasper was tired but felt an unusual sense of wellbeing. "Amazing what a difference a change of scene can make."

"Hope it wasn't just the change of scene you enjoyed?" Candy held the door open for Jasper as a matter of fact.

"Other parts of the afternoon were pleasant, too." He could not remember when he'd enjoyed himself more. It wasn't even the champagne or the kisses, or what had followed the kisses. Candy's unfailing regard gave his company a certain something that Jasper had not even realised he'd been missing. He waited for Candy to pull the door shut so they could walk up the stairs together. A small thing, but he'd discovered an appetite for Candy's proximity.

Mrs Hollins opened the door of her ground-floor sitting room. "There you are. Did you have a pleasant day in the countryside?"

Jasper turned to her with a nod. "We did—thanks to your excellent repast. Can I congratulate you on a job well done?"

Mrs Hollins beamed. "I'm glad to hear it. Captain Candy did so want everything to be nice."

Candy was a dull pink colour. He cleared his throat, stroking his thick moustache as if it were a curtain he might hide behind. "I flatter myself we succeeded."

Mrs Hollins nodded. "Oh, before I forget. Mr Carruthers, your son called."

Jasper halted, foot on the first stair. "Nigel came here?" He tasted bile in his throat, cold stealing through his veins. It had not occurred to him that Nigel would know his address.

The housekeeper nodded. "To collect the parcel you sent him for. Only, you must have forgotten to leave it out. He had to search for it."

Nigel had searched their rooms. Jasper forced himself to climb the stairs, his legs staggering below him as though disconnected from his body. He lurched into the shared sitting room.

Nigel's search had been thorough. Although he did not leave a mess, almost nothing in the sitting room stood in its usual place. Jasper scanned the room, noting that even the books in the bookcase had been removed and returned to their usual places. Nigel had left nothing unturned.

He opened the door to his bedroom and braced for the worst.

Nigel had concentrated his search here. He'd not taken as many pains to hide the evidence of his search, either. Instead, the doors of the wardrobe where he'd stowed the bag containing Aziza's casket were wide open, the missing bag plainly visible.

Jasper felt his knees wobble. He grasped the chair beside his bed, only just sinking onto it before his legs gave way altogether.

Aziza was gone—and with her, Jasper's future in the postal service.

"Is everything all right, Mr Carruthers?" Mrs Hollins

stood in the doorway of his bedroom, twisting her hands together. "He said he was your son, and the family resemblance—I never thought to question him."

"Nigel is my son." Jasper gripped the edge of his seat. The room whirled around him, a distant pounding in his ears. "He did not have my permission to take anything from my rooms, but I know from experience how determined he can be. Do not reprimand yourself, Mrs Hollins." Nigel was only doing what his role as postmaster demanded, and his discovery and seizure of Aziza would no doubt justify his deception in the eyes of the law.

"You heard the man." Candy shooed Mrs Hollins out of the room. "Leave this to me. I'll get it sorted out in no time."

Jasper heard the door close behind the landlady and the clink of glasses in the other room. He shut his eyes. Candy, for all his good intentions and regard, could not make this right.

A dreadful thought occurred to him. He lurched across the room, pulling out his bottom drawer. He felt under the drawer liner. The hard edge of an envelope met his fingertips. He had not found the letter.

Jasper swallowed. There was little consolation to be had there. With Aziza, Nigel had found everything he needed to destroy his father.

"Here." Candy was at his side, a glass of brandy in his hand. "Drink this."

"It will not do any good. She's gone—he's taken her, Rudy."

Candy took Jasper's hand and wrapped his fingers around the glass. He pushed him back over to the seat. "Drink. You'll feel better, and we can figure this out."

"The only thing you must figure out is how to find a new room-mate to cover my half of the rent." Jasper sipped the brandy. The sting was a welcome counterbalance to the buzzing in his head. He took another, longer sip. "This is the proof he's been searching for."

"Nigel's your son?" Candy frowned. "What does he intend to do with Aziza?"

"Ruin me." Jasper's fingers tightened around the glass. "Nigel is the postmaster of the General Post Office—second only to the postmaster general in authority."

"Good heavens," Candy repeated. "And his search here—"

"I disobeyed post office protocol in bringing Aziza's casket to my private residence. Nigel's been searching for proof that I'm unfit to carry on working for the postal service. This is the proof he needs."

"Come now, man! Don't surrender without a battle!" Candy patted him on his shoulder. "What about your years of service? It should be obvious to all the effort you put into your work—not to mention, if you hadn't taken Aziza home she might have been stolen by that Angel chap!"

Jasper smiled thinly. "The postmaster general won't see it like that. I'm afraid that I must resign myself to the loss of my job—and my good name." He could expect no mercy from Nigel.

"Hogwash!" Candy thundered. "Codswallop! You're the best man I know—and I'm not standing by to see you robbed of your reputation when everything you've done has been with others in mind! No—we're not taking this sitting down."

Jasper blinked. Candy could not be serious. "You must see that this is hopeless. Your reputation at the museum—if your superiors find out you're associating with a man accused of theft from the postal service…"

"You haven't been accused yet." Candy stomped out of the room. He returned with Jasper's coat and hat, which he all but threw at Jasper. "There's still time. Let's talk to Angel. It's about time he took responsibility for his actions. I'm not letting a good man go down because he was too kind-hearted."

Jasper's fingers closed around his coat. His heart thudded in his chest, not with pleasant warmth as it had that afternoon, nor even with the fear of minutes ago. This was different. Candy had somehow roused his fighting instincts.

He stood, pulling on his coat. "You're right. I must speak to Angel. But I shall do so alone."

Candy blinked at him. "Alone? Jasper—"

"Carruthers." This hurt, but it was necessary—like an incision a surgeon made to spare the patient greater pain. Jasper spoke rapidly. "I am grateful for your regard for me, and I am not insensible to your charms or those of your friendship. But I must do this alone." He swallowed. "When I am in your presence, I forget myself, giving way to my instincts. I cannot afford to be swayed by instinct now."

Candy stared at him. "What are you saying, man?"

"You know how I desire harmony." Jasper took a deep breath. "This requires me to be in complete control of my thoughts and actions. When I confront Angel, I must be in complete command. When you're with me, I err on the side of reckless abandon."

Candy smirked at him. "You certainly do."

This was not going as Jasper had intended. He felt himself turning pink, the memory of that reckless abandon that very afternoon still fresh. "I cannot allow a bad influence on my self-control such as yourself to sway my actions."

Candy smirked. "You did not mind my bad influence earlier. In fact, I seem to remember that you were quite forward in getting what you wanted."

"That is the problem. If we had not dallied in the woods, if we had caught our train and returned on time, we might have prevented Nigel from taking Aziza."

"There's no guarantee of that." Candy pulled on his coat.

"I agree that the situation is dire, but I am not letting you take the fall for another man's mistakes."

"But I—"

Candy turned, giving Jasper a stern look. "Are you arguing with me? That is not harmonious behaviour, Private."

He should have resisted, argued, and quietly but firmly disentangled himself from Candy and his ridiculous conceits.

He certainly should not have kissed Candy on his weather-beaten cheek. "Reporting for duty, sir."

21

A ngel opened the back door of 14 Trent Street with no surprise. "So, you're here at last." He stepped back, allowing them into the kitchen.

Jasper scanned the kitchen. It was outfitted well, with copper pots and pans hanging on the walls, and a modern gas range replacing the fireplace of times past. However, the pans had a dull look, and the benches bare in a manner that spoke more of disuse than of careful cleaning.

Angel himself did not look well. The red rims around his eyes and the thinness of his cheeks told their own story. "I don't even care anymore," he said. "It's all the same. Whether it's you or Lord Cross, I'm not getting out of this."

Candy tensed beside Jasper. "What kind of attitude is that? Pull yourself together, man! Have a little self-respect."

Angel gaped at him.

Jasper permitted himself a smile. Candy's spirit was such that he could not stand to see surrender in any form—not even in a man that he'd spent the entire journey to Trent Street denouncing as a villain. "Believe it or not, Mr Angel, we're here to help. Suppose you tell us the whole story about the stone you took from the casket."

As Candy bustled about the kitchen, finding the means to make a pot of tea and making sharp remarks about the state of the place, Angel told his story. "Our parents are proud folk. Couldn't abide the shame of having an unmarried daughter with child. And Mary, she was such a sweet girl. Good-natured to a fault. She's not the first girl to have been taken advantage of by a man who made promises he had no intent on delivering."

"Not at all." Men as a group had a lot to answer for. "So, Mary came to you for help."

"She was desperate," Angel said. "And who could blame her? Few would employ a ruined woman. Lord Cross wasn't likely to visit for a while, so I saw no harm in putting her up in one of the empty maid's rooms. She even gave me a hand with the linen and the polishing. And then—something went wrong. She couldn't feel the babe anymore." Angel stared at Jasper. "I don't know if you can imagine the terror she felt at that. My salary wasn't due until the end of the quarter. I had to do something."

"You did what any brother would," Jasper assured him.

Angel's shoulders slumped forward. He leaned on his elbows, his face buried in his hands. "The crate was there. I knew Lord Cross and Mr Leighton were not expected for months. Lots of time for me to pawn whatever was in it, pay for Mary's hospital care, and then raise the money to redeem it. I had no idea what I was meddling with. The cat—" He gave a choking sob. "That damnable cat!"

Out of the corner of his eye, Jasper saw Candy stiffen. He spoke quickly, hoping to avoid a scene. "You removed a stone from the casket and pawned it. And the cat made her presence known after this?"

He nodded. "It never left me alone. Haunting me. I thought I'd lost it and then it would press up against me. I got desperate. Lord Cross was expected in town, so I returned the crate to sender, hoping it would get lost. But it came back—I couldn't escape it." He raised his weary gaze to Jasper. "You brought it back."

"What you're admitting to is a very serious offence," Jasper said. "Stealing from your employer, not to mention Her Majesty's Postal Service. However, although I cannot condone your actions, I can sympathise with your loss." He looked to Candy. "My companion has a suggestion to put before you."

Candy placed a steaming cup of tea before Angel. "The day is not lost."

Angel stared at the cup before him. He looked more toad-like than ever, his hollow cheeks exacerbating the clammy appearance of his skin. "I'm willing to give myself up. I have no means with which to redeem the stone. Everything I had, I lost at cards."

"Hear us out," Jasper said. "Candy's proposal is unortho-dox, but it just might work."

Candy nodded. "I'm familiar with the sort of gaming house you frequented. They're worked by professional sharks whose aim is to fleece desperate souls. You probably did pretty well for a start. Won the first game, the second—even the third. Then your luck changed."

Angel stared at him. A dull pink infused his cheeks. "How did you know?"

"Captain Candy is very well travelled," Jasper said. "He has rubbed shoulders with all elements of society, from the well-heeled to the less reputable."

"I'm familiar with the tricks these fellows employ." Candy drew his chair up to the table. "I propose the three of us give these chaps a taste of their own medicine."

Jasper nodded. "We fleece them at cards, winning back enough for you to redeem the stone. You return it to me, and the post office delivers Mr Leighton his property intact, with no one the wiser as to its little adventure."

Angel gaped at them. His open mouth gave him the air of

one gathering flies—particularly unfortunate with his glassy eyes. "You'd do this for me? Why? I don't deserve this."

"Your sister did not deserve the treatment she received, either." Jasper coughed, removing his spectacles. He wiped them with his handkerchief, avoiding looking at either of his companions. "I have lost a child in similar circumstances. I know your pain."

Angel transferred his gaze to Candy.

He snorted. "I'm just here to make sure that Carruthers doesn't get into any more trouble on your behalf. He's done a great deal for you—much more than you deserve, if you ask me."

"But you'd still help me." Angel downed his cup of tea in one gulp. "All right. I'm in."

Jasper's chest tightened. They were committed now.

"Excellent stuff." Candy slapped Angel on the back. "Here's my plan. You introduce Carruthers to your so-called friends, indicating that he's willing to put up your opening bid. It will be apparent at a glance to anyone that Mr Carruthers rarely patronises such establishments. To the gambling sharks, he will appear a prime victim for their scheme. Mr Carruthers, you will not, I hope, object to furthering that impression with a few foolhardy observations?"

"I daresay I can manage."

"I will join your game in the guise of a stranger to you both," Candy continued. "They will not suspect collusion between us."

"And will we be colluding?" Jasper asked with dismay.

Candy nodded. "There is nothing honourable about these men, nor the games they play. If we are to extricate Mr Angel from this mess, we cannot afford to be too nice in our methods."

"Come to think of it," Angel intoned. "It does seem a bit

too convenient that my luck changed so dramatically—and so consistently."

Candy nodded. "As I said, I know the type only too well. Now, here's what I propose. One of the camp attendants back in my army days moonlighted at a bar in Cairo. He taught me how they fix the games." He took a battered deck of cards from his jacket. "Here's what we will do."

22

It took four hours of drilling before Candy was satisfied that Angel and Jasper would pass muster at the bar. It was approaching midnight as Angel guided Jasper into the gaming house, as Candy termed the bar. Jasper looked around with distaste, holding his handkerchief over his mouth to stop himself from breathing in the thick smoke and the sour smell that underlay it.

"Over here." Angel led the way to a table at the very back of the bar. Two men looked up from their beers. Their beards were stained with smoke, and their eyes gleamed in the dim light, lingering on Jasper's coat. One had a red bandana around his neck, the other, a scar that ran the length of his cheek. Both looked lean and hungry, like greyhounds.

Angel slung himself into a chair. "I want a rematch."

"Sure you do," Bandana said. "And I want a cottage in the countryside, but we're neither of us getting it, are we?"

"You're broke," Scar agreed. "Come back when you've got something worth rolling for."

Angel jerked his thumb over his shoulder. "He'll cover me."

It took everything in Jasper not to recoil at the predatory

looks he received. He felt weighed and valued, from his crisp gloves to his polished coat buttons to his boots.

The two men exchanged a look. "Always nice to meet a friend of Angel's." Bandana held out a hand. "You'll join us? Drinks on us."

Jasper returned the handshake. "How very pleasant. I should be delighted." He perched on the edge of his chair. "And how does one play cards? I confess, I know very little of the pastime."

The grin that passed between the two men deserved the term 'shark-like.' "You'll pick it up in no time," Scar told him. "Just wait and see."

Jasper sipped his beer—a potent brew for something that tasted so weak—and squinted at the cards he held. "The jack is an odd-looking fellow, isn't he? I don't think I care for that moustache."

The glee on Bandana's face was indecent. "You'll soon appreciate the jack. You get a pair of those, you're doing well."

Somehow, despite Jasper's complete ignorance, the fact that he put his hand down face-up on the table to mop up a bit of spilt beer, and paused to consult Angel as to how he should play his cards several times, he ended up scooping the pot. "It really is easier than you think."

"You're a natural," Scar assured him, reshuffling the cards. "Another game?"

"If you insist." Jasper picked up his cards with confidence. He'd spotted Candy in his peripheral vision, slouched against the wall. As Scar got to work dealing out the cards, Bandana began telling a bawdy story.

Jasper paid close attention to the words. The two men must have some means of communicating. Words—or some form of signal? He made a series of hopeless errors, discarding high-value cards and picking at random from the deck. And yet, once again, he produced the winning hand.

"Marvellous," Bandana congratulated him. "You've got an instinct for the game. Not many people do."

Scar nodded. "I propose we make things a little more interesting. What do you say to raising the stakes?"

This time, Jasper lost—but not by much.

Bandana made no move to scoop up his winnings. "What do you gentlemen say to joining me in another round? Drinks on me."

"Allow me." Candy inserted himself between Bandana and Scar, tossing a pouch onto the table. It crunched as it hit the wood. Scar's eyes glittered. He made way for Candy at once.

He would be much less enthusiastic if he knew the pouch contained the metal weights used by cooks to shape their pastry. Jasper coughed, polishing his glasses. "Well, I don't know… It is rather late…."

"You must stay," Angel insisted, eying the money on the table. "Just one more game."

"Since this is the last, we'll make it worth it." Scar put down a pile of coins and Bandana added a sovereign. "What do you say? You in, gentlemen?"

With a show of unwillingness, Jasper placed a sovereign on the table. He'd emptied his wallet. He had to trust that Candy knew what he was doing. "Very well."

The game was soon underway. Jasper sensed a different undercurrent to it. Bandana talked less, but when he did his words were rapid-fire, his laugh forced. Scar scratched his head so often that Jasper might have suspected he had lice if it were not for the fact the gestures proceeded every bid Bandana made.

Jasper's comments met with little response. When at last the time came to show their hands, Candy was on top.

He gathered up the pot, calculating his winnings. Angel watched him, fingers clamped tight around the handle of his tankard.

Jasper could guess what he was thinking. Did they have enough to redeem the stone?

"Another game?" Scar said. "Night's still young."

Candy nodded. "All right."

They were still short—and now they'd shown their hand. Jasper willed himself to remain calm. "I'm out, I'm afraid. This wasn't how I expected to end my night."

Angel clutched at Jasper's coat. "Your watch."

"I beg your pardon!" They'd discussed this as a potential ploy to ensure that the sharks did not suspect that they were working in tandem with Candy.

"I promise you, I'll get it back." Angel painted a compelling picture of a desperate man. The dull light of the bar gleamed on his clammy skin.

"Very well—but this is the last." Jasper set the watch down.

Angel picked up the cards dealt him, but Jasper shook his head.

"Another round!" Bandana signalled the bartender. Drinks were placed on the table and the men got down to the serious business of playing.

Jasper picked up his tankard but did not try to drink it. He'd already been forgotten. Bandana and Scar were focused on divesting Candy of his winnings. Scar scratched his temple. Candy's eyes flashed, meeting Jasper's for a brief moment.

So, Candy had not failed to notice the gesture. Jasper tried to keep his inner elation from showing on his face. While Jasper had been playing the part of a novice, Candy had ample opportunity to study Scar and Bandana's methods. The two men had no idea how thoroughly they'd been played.

Or did they?

As Jasper's glance fell on Bandana, he saw him lift his hand away from the rim of a tankard. He shifted the pitcher closer to Candy. In a neat gesture—so quick that if Jasper had blinked, he'd have missed it—he uplifted Candy's glass, leaving his pitcher in its place.

The strange potency of his weak beer took on a new significance. Jasper glanced at Candy, but he was looking at his cards, oblivious to the substitution. Angel was likewise focused on the game.

Jasper gripped the side of his chair, endeavouring to keep his agitation in check. The success of their wild plan depended on him controlling himself. He must trust Candy and Angel to play their parts. Everything depended on it.

Candy grunted in response to a remark Bandana made. He reached for the tankard without looking up from his cards. He raised it to his lips—

Jasper's hand shot out. He caught Candy's wrist before he could taste the drink.

The game halted instantly.

Jasper could feel Bandana and Scar staring at him. He released Candy's hand, sitting down. "Terribly sorry, but if I'm not mistaken that drink has been tampered with."

"Here!" Scar pushed back his chair and stood. "What's the meaning of this?"

The bar was so quiet they might have heard a pin drop.

"I should ask *you* that question." Jasper tried not to notice that several of the bar patrons were moving towards them. "What did you put in his drink?"

"You're mistaken," Bandana said. "Imagining things, old man."

Candy picked up the tankard. "He is imagining nothing. This isn't my drink!"

A broad-shouldered man loomed over their table. "It seems like you're having a spot of trouble, gentlemen?" The apron he wore over his clothes was stained, and Jasper didn't think all those marks were spilt drinks.

"Nothing to worry about," Bandana said. "This chap has had too much to drink and is confused."

"I object!" Jasper indicated his tankard. "I have hardly touched my drink—and a good thing, too. It tasted jolly peculiar—"

Angel leaned forward, scooping the takings off the table and into his suit pockets.

"What are you doing? Here!" Candy scrambled to his feet as Angel ducked into the crowd. "Come back! We haven't finished the game!"

As Candy plunged after Angel, Bandana started after him. Jasper saw something metal catch the dull light of the bar's lanterns. His heart lurched. "Stop that man! He has a knife!"

The man in the apron moved forward, grabbing Bandana's hand and twisting it. The knife dropped to the floor.

Bandana swore, twisting to slam his fist into the man's stomach. He might as well have been punching a wall. The man bore the attack without blinking, retaliating with a blow that sent Bandana crashing backwards into a table of spectators.

As the table tipped, drinks spilling across the floor, the room erupted into chaos. Bandana grappled with a man intent on wringing the value of his spilt drink out of him, his companions split between defending Bandana and urging their friend on. Others saw an opportunity to strike at the apron-clad man. He met their attacks unconcerned, dealing back as good as he got.

Angel fought to free himself from the grip of a group of men, clearly sticklers for the rules of fair play. Candy was likewise held back by those sympathetic to Angel's plight. He defended himself with a pragmatic blow, then charged head-first into his opponents.

"No, no, no!" Jasper crouched beneath the table. A glass smashed on the floor, adding broken glass and ale to the mix.

His head whirled, the violence he saw before him mingling with the memory of his father seizing the poker, and himself, helpless, watching as his father dealt the fatal blow…

He felt something wet on his cheeks. Tears? Terror seized his mind. He could not move. He could barely even breathe.

Out of the corner of his eye, he saw a hand reach for the knife that Bandana had dropped. Scar slunk through the bar, sidestepping a struggling pair. He raised the knife, taking careful aim at his target—Candy's back.

Jasper was moving before he knew what he was doing. He tackled Scar from behind, clinging to him like a child receiving a piggyback ride from their father. He grabbed the wrist that held the knife, trying to twist it as he had seen the apron-clad man do.

Scar roared with fury. He staggered backwards, slamming into a wall.

The force of the blow jarred every bone in Jasper's body, but he clung on, even as Scar slammed him into the wall once, twice more.

The third time Jasper's grip came loose. He slid down Scar's back, landing in a dazed heap on the floor.

Move. He had to get away. But his body did not obey him.

A sharp pain flooded his chest as Scar's boot connected with his ribs. Jasper curled up with a moan. He was helpless to defend himself—helpless, just as his mother had been.

Jasper lay on cold stone. He did not need to open his eyes to know where he was. The chill air and the putrid smell of desperation and despair were known to him from nightmare. The only difference was that this was real.

Jail. He swallowed back a sob. If he'd learned one thing from visiting his father, it was that convicts pounced on any sign of fear or weakness.

What was he but weak? Jasper tasted blood. He did not remember the cut lip. There were a lot of aches he did not remember. His transportation to the prison cell was a hazy memory. In fact, the only thing he remembered was the horror of seeing Scar take aim at Candy—

Candy! Jasper opened his eyes. With effort, he heaved himself into a sitting position.

He was in a large holding cell, the number of benches insufficient for the number of men within. Those lucky enough to score a bench slept or at least reclined. The remainder lay on the stone, like Jasper, or leaned against the walls. A thick wooden door with an iron grill marked the only entrance or exit, a second metal grill in the wall providing the only source of fresh air and light.

Jasper scanned the cell. He recognised some of the men from the brawl. Scar and Bandana were not among those present—but neither were Candy nor Angel.

Angel. Jasper's mouth tasted sour. He'd shown no compunctions about running, leaving Candy and Jasper to deal with the mess he'd left behind. So much for trying to help the man! Candy's prediction had come true: Jasper's efforts to help had only got him into further difficulties.

And Candy… Candy's absence was the even greater blow. Had he left Jasper behind to get taken by the police, knowing how much Jasper feared this?

Jasper reached into his pocket for his handkerchief. He felt in his breast pocket for his spectacles, but when he pulled them out, the glass of one lens was cracked, the frame twisted. They had not survived the brawl.

Jasper's hand closed around the spectacles. He would not survive this. Once he failed to show up for work, Nigel would hear of it, and he would want to know why. Once news of his arrest reached Nigel, he would waste no time in informing the postmaster general. Brawling in a tavern was not the behaviour expected of those who wore the uniform of Her Majesty's Postal Service. Jasper had lost everything.

The men in the cell seemed preoccupied with their own situations. A few sat in pairs, discussing their options in low voices. Most seemed reconciled to a long wait. None tried to speak to Jasper, for which he was grateful. He took off his jacket, wincing at the state of it, and folded it into a pillow. He endeavoured, not to sleep—his body hurt too much for that—but to rest.

Sometime later, a uniformed constable unlocked the wooden door. He called out a handful of names, Jasper's among them. In company with the others called, Jasper made his way down a corridor to the police station office where a handful of civilians waited. Patience stood among them, the neatness of her brown silk dress and combed hair a striking contrast to the chaos surrounding them.

Jasper would have given anything to return to the cell. "Patience. You don't mean to say you paid my bail?"

Patience's expression tightened. She stepped forward, ignoring Jasper's protest as she touched his cheek. "Look at you! Have you seen a doctor?" She glared at the constable. "I consider this an outrageous dereliction of duty! It should be obvious to anyone that my husband is not a threat to anyone —that a man of his years should not receive a medical opinion is gross neglect!"

Jasper shut his eyes. His shame was complete. "Please, Patience. Let's leave."

She insisted on taking him home, Jasper too exhausted to protest. Patience bathed his wounds herself, bandaging his bruises and applying a poultice of her own making to the worst of them. By the time she was finished, Jasper felt even more tired.

"There." Patience turned the mirror towards him. "I've done what I can. What you need now is a strong dose of laudanum and a good sleep."

Jasper traced his fingers across the purple shadow that spread across one cheek. He was almost unrecognisable— Patience had cut his hair to minister to the cut on his temple. His jacket had been removed as damaged beyond repair, and he stood in shirtsleeves and cuffs. "Oh dear."

"I didn't believe the constable when he called, at first." Patience wound up the roll of bandages she'd used. "I told him he was mad. Of all the men to instigate a brawl in a London tavern, my Jasper would be the last."

He winced. "There were, ah, circumstances."

"There would have to be." Patience paused, looking Jasper over. She stepped forward, putting her arms around in a loose hug. "After all this time, you found something worth fighting for."

Jasper opened his mouth to protest. Angel was gone, and there had been no word from Candy. He'd been duped, his dislike of conflict causing him to put himself out there for men who had abandoned him to his worst fears. And yet—

He had found something worth fighting for. Jasper felt something unfurl deep in his chest. He squeezed Patience's hand. "It appears I have." And, having fought once, he was certain he could do it again. "What is the time? Is the post office still open?"

Patience frowned at him. "You can't be thinking of going to work."

"There is something I need to do—something I should have done many years ago." Jasper hesitated. "Will you come with me?"

She nodded. "Of course."

~

They made their way to the post office after a brief detour to Jasper's apartment so he could get a jacket and retrieve the letter. Patience waited in the sitting room, studying Candy's collection of foreign curiosities, but she made no remark. Of Candy himself, there was no sign.

Jasper felt unease. Had something happened to Candy following the brawl? There were many reasons he might not have shown up in the police cell—none of which were good.

Later, Jasper told himself. He must deal with the post office first. Then he would be free to find Candy.

As Jasper and Patience walked through the long halls of the General Post Office, Jasper discerned a hush creep over his colleagues. Rumour spread through the post office faster than the mail did. News of his disgrace was already rampant —and his present appearance did not help any. "I must apologise for making you a spectacle, my dear. I have made a mistake in judgement, and the consequences will embarrass us both."

Patience managed to snort without losing any of her ladylike dignity. "I am equal to a little embarrassment."

She was, too. Jasper felt a wave of mortification. He had been wrong—so very wrong—to not trust her with his decision.

Nigel's secretary looked up as Jasper and Patience approached. "The postmaster is currently engaged with the postmaster general—" He trailed off as he recognised Jasper.

"I imagine that I am the subject of that conversation. Don't get up—I'll let us in." Jasper rapped on the door and opened it. "After you."

Following Patience into the room, Jasper did not see the initial shock on the faces of those within. Nigel glanced from his mother to his father with a suspicious frown, while Raikes's brow tightened.

No doubt Raikes had already been treated to Nigel's version of events. "Forgive the intrusion, Postmaster General, Postmaster Carruthers. Am I wrong in my assumption you are discussing my recent actions?"

"No, indeed." Raikes was first to recover, his stern expression giving his full beard biblical overtones. "I have to say, I am dismayed by the account of your activity that I have received."

Jasper bowed. "I am here to account for my behaviour, to confess my wrongs, and to take the punishment due me."

Nigel sneered. "A confession that has come too late to do you any good! If you think that by bringing your wife into this that you will escape consequences—"

"Not at all," Jasper interposed. "As my behaviour reflects on us both, I have brought her here that she might be acquainted with all the facts." He pulled out the seat before the desk for Patience to seat herself. "May I give my account of my actions?"

Raikes nodded to Patience, stroking his long beard. "Please. I hope that you can shed some light on what seems like an extraordinary dereliction of duty."

"I shall do my best." Jasper took a deep breath. He looked at the group before him. Patience, her usual expression of calm not entirely hiding the worry in her eyes. Raikes, as stern as a page from *The Illustrated Old Testament*. Nigel, his eyes glinting, eager to pounce on any admission of guilt. The courage that had so far sustained Jasper ebbed, leaving in its place a rising tide of nausea—

Jasper shut his eyes. The memory of Candy petting an invisible cat came to mind, and he smiled, remembering once again why he'd done this. "Before I worked in the Dead Letter Office, I was assigned to work as a special agent. I did not, I'm afraid, distinguish myself. My short time investigating mail fraud not only revealed to me the extraordinary measures taken to subvert the mail but the desperate circumstances that prompted these criminal acts. I believe it was that knowledge that prompted me to take the current matter into my own hands, rather than referring it to the police. It started with the return of the crate addressed to P. Leighton, Foxwood Court…"

24

Jasper outlined the steps he'd taken to investigate the origins of the crate and return it to its rightful owner, including taking the casket home rather than risk its theft, his visit to the museum, the discovery of the missing stone, and his sighting of Angel at the hospital. He omitted any reference to Aziza herself.

"Enough!" Nigel slammed a hand against his desk. "Postmaster General, there is no need to listen any further. Carruthers admits that he—a former special agent, no less— contrived to let a thief escape judgement! He has brought the post office into disrepute and prevented the course of justice. There is no explanation he can offer that can justify such behaviour—"

Raised voices sounded outside. Raikes frowned. "It seems, Postmaster Carruthers, that there is a matter needing your attention."

As Nigel turned towards the door, it burst open. Candy strode in, sporting a vibrant bruise on one cheek and a triumphant expression. One sleeve of his jacket had been torn off and he had lost his hat and one boot. Still, as his gaze fell on Jasper, he seemed to expand. He strode across the room, oblivious to the curious stares he was getting, and pulled a small object, wrapped in brown paper, from his breast pocket. "Got it."

Jasper took the package. "Postmaster Carruthers alleges that I have brought the post office into disrepute. The honour of the post office has always been of great importance to me—second only to the importance of seeing that every piece of mail in our hands reaches its rightful owner." He unwrapped the package, revealing a stone of vivid turquoise, carved into the shape of a scarab. "It will not take a collector of Mr Leighton's repute long to realise that his property is missing a valuable stone. Once he corresponds with the gift giver, he will learn that the stone went missing here in England. It is in the interests of the post office that we ensure that no blame falls upon any innocent members of the mail service. We must safeguard our honour by returning Mr Leighton's property in pristine condition."

Raikes looked to Nigel. "Where is the casket now?"

Nigel stared at the stone. "I had it delivered to Mr Leighton at once."

Jasper sighed. "A pity. I was hoping to avoid this eventuality."

"I bet you were." Nigel clenched his fists. "Hoping to avoid it coming to light that you had taken the casket for your own ends! Once the casket was apparently stolen, you knew you could pilfer it with no suspicion falling on yourself. You sought the stone, not to return it to the owner as you claim, but because you knew the casket would be more valuable intact—"

"Shut your mouth, you impudent rapscallion!" Candy roared. "Your father has gone to immense pains to track down this stone. I'll not stand by and hear him maligned by a mingy little bootlicker like yourself!"

If enjoying the shocked expression on Nigel's face made

Jasper a bad father, then he would plead guilty. He turned to Raikes. "My departmental record speaks for itself, Postmaster General. You know the pains I take over every piece of mail that comes my way—to an extent that has sometimes been described as excessive by my colleagues, it is true. You know, too, that I am not motivated by monetary gain. I have turned down offers of promotion that were accompanied by an increase in salary. Finally, there are my actions. After I took the casket to my apartment—an action I fully admit was contrary to our regulations, and for which my good intentions do not offer adequate excuse—I did not abandon my attempts to discover Mr Leighton. I had an interview with him only yesterday, in which I ascertained his credentials as the true owner of the casket, and his address."

Jasper nodded to Candy. "Captain Candy accompanied me on this trip and, as you have no doubt inferred, aided me in the restoration of the stone. With your permission, Postmaster General, I should like to return the stone to Mr Leighton personally, putting forward the complete facts of the case as I do." He cleared his throat. "The interview will be a delicate one, requiring a great deal of tact and diplomacy, with the reputation of the post office at stake. I consider myself equal to the task."

"As do I." Raikes nodded his head. "Should you succeed in clearing this matter up, the post office will owe you a great debt of service. Postmaster Carruthers, on the other hand..." He turned his stern gaze on Nigel.

His son took a step back, his hands clutching at his throat. His lips were pale. "I did only what I thought was best, Postmaster General."

"And you have brought the post office to the brink of scandal in the process. I am very disappointed in you, Postmaster Carruthers. In fact, I should like to see your uniform and a letter proffering your resignation on my desk by the end of the day."

Nigel staggered back into his chair.

Jasper coughed. "Please do not judge Postmaster Carruthers too harshly, sir. The role of postmaster requires a breadth of experience, not merely in matters connected to the post but in, ah, human experience, too. One must be able to see beyond the surface appearance to a full understanding of the people beneath. Postmaster Carruthers is very capable, but he has a lot to learn about trust, tact, and delicacy. Might I suggest that he spend some time in the Dead Letter Office? I have found it an excellent classroom of human foibles, and it should delight me to share with him the benefit of my experience. It would be a shame to lose so promising a postmaster to a youthful mistake."

Raikes stroked his beard. "Very well. I will accept your suggestion, Department Head Carruthers."

Jasper licked his lips. Reinstated! "Thank you, sir."

Raikes looked to Nigel. "Carruthers, you have until the end of today to clear out your office." He gave Candy, Patience, and Jasper a quick nod and stalked out of the room.

Jasper breathed out. That had gone much better than he had expected it to.

"I suppose you're pleased with yourself." Nigel raised his head to glare at him.

"Yes—but not for the reason you might think." Jasper patted his pocket, pulling out his spectacles. He turned over the broken glasses before tucking them away again. "It shall be my pleasure to instruct you in the proper investigation of dead mail—and to get to know my son." He paused. "Nigel, you accused me of putting my career before my family. You were right. I neglected my family, but it was not ambition or pride that motivated me, but fear—a fear that I should have known was ill-founded by your excellent mother's strength of character. It is time you know all."

Patience looked up at him, her clear eyes waiting. Nigel stared at him like one dazed.

Candy cleared his throat. "I'll step outside—"

"Stay." Jasper took a deep breath. "It is just as well you know the worst of me." He took the letter from his jacket pocket. "I have always had a horror of argument. Nothing is more distasteful to me than disagreement, or the excessive passion that is so often its cause. When Patience and I married, we both knew it was not for love. Our union was founded on mutual respect, and a bond formed when we were both cast aside by a man who had once been a dear friend of us both."

"You married me to save my reputation." Patience raised her chin. "If we are to be truthful, let us not hide that fact. Our mutual friend led me to believe we were engaged, all the while courting another. He married, leaving me carrying his child and with no means of redress."

Nigel shook his head, sinking lower into his chair. "This cannot be true! Your character is above reproach—you would never allow yourself to be so debased."

"Your mother's predicament says more about her deceiver than it does about herself. She made the best of a poor situation," Jasper said. "Respect is no substitute for love, but we got on tolerably, and then you came along, which was a very welcome thing. You gave us an interest. Something of your mother's old spirit came back. Your childish prattle awoke the woman she had been before our marriage. I dared to think our arrangement was no bad thing for either of us— and then, the letter."

He took it from his jacket. "It is a strange irony that of all the clerks in the post office, this landed on my desk. A letter addressed to my wife, containing a letter she'd written to our mutual friend—and his reply."

Patience caught her breath, colour flaming into her pale cheeks. "Is that—"

"The one letter that I failed to deliver." Jasper nodded to Nigel. "I hope it is some consolation to know that your suspicions about me were correct, even if you were wrong about my motivations." He took a deep breath. "It was a shock to know that my wife was corresponding with a man she professed to despise—more so, that she had hidden this from me. I could not help but wonder what else she hid. The respect that had been the foundation of our marriage was no more. I could not bear to see it degrade further. It was at this point that I removed myself, hoping that in my absence, Patience would find the happiness she desired and so deserved." He held out the letter. "I regret not giving this to you sooner, my dear. I should have known better."

Patience took it, turning it over. "I had heard that Walter and his wife were back in England. I wrote to him to inform him that our child had not survived—he had a right to know. He wrote back." Her lip curled. "He expressed neither sorrow nor pity. Instead, he talked about how empty his marriage was, how much he missed me. He claimed to still have feelings for me. Would I meet him again?" She crumpled the letter in her fist. "The part of me that had once loved him was revolted. Did he think so little of me—of Jasper—that he would propose such a thing? I could not let this insult go unanswered. I replied, agreeing to a meeting. It was my intention to charge him with his ungentlemanly behaviour, let him see how much I loathed him. He did not reply. I decided that his desire to see me again was nothing more than a whim." She bowed her head. "It was a dark time, made darker by the fact that my best friend held himself at such a distance. But my freedom was a source of solace of its own. Caring for you, Nigel, occupied my days and in time, I found fresh occupation. I cannot blame you from not trusting me, Jasper, when I was the first to keep secrets."

Jasper squeezed her hand. "Are we friends again, my dear?"

She smiled at him, tucking the crumpled letter up her sleeve. "We are."

"Good." Jasper picked up the stone. "Candy and I will deliver this to Mr Leighton. Nigel, I shall expect to see you tomorrow at ten o'clock sharp." Jasper turned to Candy. "Shall we?"

Candy's good eye gleamed. "We shall."

151

25

J asper's heart sank as number 14 Trent Street came into view. Despite his assurances to the postmaster general, he was not certain that he was up to this task. He'd not forgotten what the staff at Foxwood Court had said about Lord Cross's bad temper.

"Steady, Carruthers," Candy said. "After the dressing down you gave that odious son of yours, a mere lord should be nothing."

Jasper glanced at Candy, his lips quirking. "Am I so easily read?"

Candy, to his great surprise, blushed. They'd taken the time to stop by their apartment so that Candy could change into fresh attire and Jasper could stiffen his nerves with a quick drink. They both still looked somewhat disreputable—there was not much that could be done about their bruises. "I have made rather a study of your mannerisms. I fancy I know you about as well as any man could."

A warm glow transfused Jasper. To be so regarded! "I shall have to return the favour."

"You already have." Candy squeezed his hand. "I'll never

forget what you did for me in that gaming house. You're a brave man, Carruthers, don't let anyone tell you different."

Jasper did not feel brave, but Candy's confidence buoyed him. He climbed the steps, ringing the bell of number 14. "Here we go."

Some time passed without the door being opened.

"Angel's long gone," Candy said. "He's got the wind up—he was convinced that as soon as Lord Cross heard of the matter, he'd be prosecuted. I got him to sign a confession of what he'd done in return for promising not to hand it over until his ship had sailed."

Jasper nodded. So, Candy's absence resulted from him tracking Angel down? "How did you convince him to hand over the stone?"

"No convincing necessary. He was pleased to see the back of it." Candy thumped the door. "How long do you suppose they intend to keep us waiting?"

Jasper frowned. Was anyone even resident? Leighton had spoken of his intentions to travel to London, but plans could change—

The door opened. A wan child, his suit rumpled, eyed them without curiosity.

Jasper shot Candy a puzzled glance. He leaned forward, putting himself on the child's level. "Excuse me, young man. Is Mr Leighton present?"

"He is," the boy said.

"May we see him?" Jasper prompted.

"Not if you stand there," the boy said. "Father's inside."

Candy snorted. "We want to talk to your father, young fellow. Lead us to him."

"If that's what you wanted, you should have said." The boy turned aside, leading the way into the townhouse.

Jasper followed the boy inside. Suitcases and trunks were piled in the hallway. A vase lay on its side on the floor in a puddle of flowers and water. "A spot of domestic difficulty?"

"The staff went back to the country," the boy said. "It's just me, father, and Lord Cross."

"And the cat?" Jasper guessed.

The boy turned to look back at him. There was a feline glint to his eyes. "And the cat." He opened a door, revealing not a drawing room, but a kitchen.

Mr Leighton, with his shirt sleeves rolled up to reveal his bare arms, stood over a sizzling frying pan. A haze of smoke filled the room. "It's not ready yet—" he trailed off, blinking at his guests. "Mr Carruthers, Captain Candy. I did not expect to see you so soon."

The boy lolled against the table. "They said they wanted to talk to you."

Mr Leighton grimaced, wiping his hands on the apron he wore. "I hope you don't mind, gentlemen, but we are somewhat inconvenienced right now."

Jasper and Candy exchanged a look. "Perhaps we can be of assistance?"

"I'm not sure you can. It's a rather delicate problem—" A sausage popped in the pan, and Mr Leighton jumped.

"I'll take over." Candy stepped up to the stove. "I'm an old hand at this. I'll have lunch served in half an hour." He snapped his fingers. "You, boy. Think you can rustle up an onion?"

The boy looked with fresh interest at Candy. "Do you mean find one? Because if so, yes."

"Splendid." Jasper put a hand on Mr Leighton's arm and steered him out of the kitchen. "Suppose we adjoin to somewhere a little quieter?"

Mr Leighton showed him into a sitting room where a bearded man poked at a fireplace. "No blasted luck," he reported. "Suppose we swap?" He paused as he caught sight of Jasper, getting to his feet with a glare. "We are not receiving visitors."

Facing down the postmaster general was one thing: the

glare levelled on him by Lord Cross quite another. Jasper stared at him, struggling to find an argument. "I think you'll see me, sir."

Cross snorted, crossing his arms. There was a combative glint in his eyes, and his form seemed braced for battle. A man who not only did not fear battle but who thrived on it. "I doubt that very much. On what pretext have you forced your company upon us when we are neither in the mood nor have the capacity to want it?"

A warm pressure leaned against his heels. Aziza butted her head against his leg.

Jasper knelt down, scooping the cat up. "There you are." He stroked her fur and within a few seconds, her contented purr was audible throughout the room.

"You know about the cat." Mr Leighton breathed.

"Her name is Aziza," Jasper said. "Beloved pet of Ameres, High Priest of the temple of Osiris. Captain Candy can inform you of her origins and time period better than I. She was delivered to the Dead Letter Office after the label was torn from the crate containing her, and it was there I became acquainted with her, ah, unusual nature."

Lord Cross cocked an eyebrow. "I apologise, Mr Carruthers. You may indeed be just the man we need."

"I hope so." Jasper gave Aziza a last stroke and then set her down. "In my attempts to reunite Mr Leighton's package with its rightful owner, it came to my attention that a stone of particular import was removed from her casket. Where is the casket?"

"Locked in the study," Mr Leighton said. "The staff insisted."

"I'll get it." Lord Cross strode across the room. He returned shortly thereafter, bearing the casket.

Jasper took the stone from his pocket. He felt Aziza curl around his ankles. "Good girl." He blinked. It only now struck him just how much he owed the cat.

May you find your owner. He placed the stone on the casket. It fitted into place as smoothly as a button.

Mr Leighton and Lord Cross stood still.

"I don't hear her," Mr Leighton said.

"You may have helped us a great deal, Mr—?" Lord Cross held out a hand.

"Carruthers. Jasper Carruthers, Department of Dead Letters." Jasper grimaced at the crushing handshake.

Leighton was on his knees, feeling around for the cat. "I don't feel her anywhere…"

"A glass of something is in order." Cross made his way to a sideboard where a bottle of whiskey stood ready. "If I may, Mr Carruthers, how on earth did you get hold of the stone?"

Jasper took a deep breath, his hand resting on the casket. "That is a long story."

26

Lord Cross and Mr Leighton took the news of Angel's theft and subsequent desertion well, on the whole. "Strange," Mr Leighton mused. "Of all men to have a sister, I should never suspect Angel of it."

Lord Cross snorted. The whiskey—and the fact that Aziza had made no further appearances—seemed to have a beneficial effect on his temper. "That's the bit you struggle with?"

Mr Leighton took the comment in stride. "I cannot argue with Mr Carruthers about the cat. We both felt her. And there are the corroboratory statements of the staff."

Jasper coughed. "Am I to infer that Aziza's presence led to the mass desertion of your staff?"

Lord Cross nodded. "They refused to spend the night under the same roof as the—the mummy. They have returned to Foxwood Court, on the firm understanding that the mummy is not to return to Foxwood with us."

"That's no problem," Mr Leighton's tone was cheerful. "We can keep her in London."

Lord Cross eyed him. "And who will keep *us* in London?"

The door opened. The boy entered, his cheeks glowing with pleasure. "Did you know that Captain Candy's eye is made of glass? He took it out and showed me. He said it was an accident that happened in Afghanistan and he will tell me about it when I am older, and he let me stir the frying pan and he also said to tell you that dinner is served."

"Devilled sausages," Candy said modestly. He'd not only produced dinner, but he'd laid out the table, too. "A favourite with the troops."

"We are very much in your debt. In all the excitement, we'd quite forgot luncheon." Mr Leighton waved them both towards chairs. "Mr Carruthers, Captain Candy, you'll join us?"

Jasper tugged at his tie. "We don't want to intrude."

"No intrusion, I assure you. You have done us a very great service." Mr Leighton's eyes gleamed. "I hope you'll tell us more about your experiences with Aziza."

Jasper had intended to stay only as long as was polite. Instead, it was many hours and more than a few glasses of some very fine brandy before Jasper and Candy wove their way back through the streets towards their shared apartment.

"The boy seems nice." Candy observed. "Hardly the monster you supposed. Very positively inclined towards Aziza. I fancy we have nothing to fear there."

"No," Jasper agreed. "I quite misjudged the boy. Aziza seems to have landed on her feet—or should that be paws?"

Candy cleared his throat. "On the subject of poor judgement, I apologise for what I said about your son. My temper got the better of me. It riled me to see you so disrespected."

Jasper decided he could allow himself a slight smirk. "Nigel has learnt an important lesson today. I hope that he takes it to heart."

"With such bastions of tact and thoughtfulness as his parents as role models, I am sure he cannot help but learn." Candy glanced at Jasper. "Your wife is a very attractive woman."

Jasper pressed his lips together. "She is."

"She doesn't seem to hold a grudge against your treatment of her. In fact, she seems rather fond of you." Candy hunched his shoulders. "What I mean to say is, if there is any chance of a reconciliation... well, I wouldn't want to stand in the way."

Jasper shook his head. "Walter would always be between us."

"Walter." Candy scowled. "I've never met a Walter I didn't dislike. This man sounds an absolute bounder! He's not worth a second thought."

"It's not Walter himself. I was fond of him once—very fond—but his treatment of Patience put an end to my regard for him. No, it's what happened to Walter." Jasper cast a sideways look at Candy. "Were you in England for the Mitford murder?"

"No, but I heard about it," Candy said. "The chap's skull is part of the British Museum's collection. Donated—we're not in the habit of collecting such sordid specimens." He caught his breath. "That chap was a Walter. You don't mean to say—"

"Our mutual friend." Jasper came to a stop before the steps of their lodgings. "He told his wife he'd been called away on business and booked a room in a quiet country hotel. He had one caller—a veiled woman whose visit lasted less than half an hour. The innkeeper discovered him the next day, stabbed through the heart, and, ah... divested of a certain part of his anatomy. It came out after his death that he'd carried on his amorous ways, even after his marriage. He'd had more than one mistress, all of whom had alibis for the time of his death. No one was ever charged with his death, and the mysterious woman visitor never identified. It was supposed that she was the mother or sister of one of the women he had so callously ruined, or even a husband or lover in disguise."

Candy stared at him. "You can't think..."

"Patience is the last woman I would accuse of such a thing," Jasper said quietly. "But she was forced to conceal her pregnancy while Walter celebrated his marriage. The doctor told us that stress had likely contributed to the loss of the baby. The place that Patience set for their assignation was Mitford, the date, the day on which Walter died."

"Good heavens," Candy repeated. "That is—"

"A very odd coincidence," Jasper said firmly. "One that I'm sure many people would put a sordid interpretation on. I decided not to look into it any further." He'd intended to stop there, but Candy's gaze resting on him prompted him to continue. "If I'd found proof, I'd have had to do something about it. But I saw what prison did to a hard man like my father. I could not endure the thought of Patience subjected to that fate—but neither do I have any inclination to share my mother's fate, either. I will continue to live alone."

"Not entirely alone, I hope." Candy tugged his moustache. "I continue to find our arrangement suitable, and today's disclosures have not altered my opinion of you one iota."

Jasper breathed out. He had not detected any censure from Candy, but knowing their friendship was secure was a relief unlike any other. "Then I shall be happy to remain your room-mate."

The word was entirely inadequate for the understanding between them, but from the way Candy blinked, Jasper knew that his message had been delivered.

The evening was chill, but the sitting room of 14 Trent Street was pleasantly warm. Lord Cross, finishing the chapter of the book he was perusing, looked up, intending to remark on the contrast of the comfort of their present arrangements to those of the afternoon. Instead, his attention was caught by the posture of his adopted son.

Julian sprawling in front of the fireplace was nothing new. Julian, lying with his chin resting on his folded arms, eyes fixed on an empty spot in front of him, was.

Cross leaned over and patted Pip's arm. As he looked up in enquiry, Cross motioned to their son.

Pip's eyes widened. He put down the collection of folklore he was reading. "Julian—can you see the cat?"

Julian shook his head, not moving his gaze from the patch of carpet he was studying. "No. But I can see where she ought to be."

Pip followed his gaze to the empty carpet. He put his book aside and knelt on the carpet, stretching out a hand. "There she is." He ran his hand through the empty air. "You're a friendly cat, aren't you?"

An audible meow answered.

Cross winced. "That's going to be hard to explain to the housemaids."

"Imagination," Pip said, continuing to stroke the invisible cat. "Or the neighbours' cat. They have a cat, don't they?"

Cross snorted. "I'm surprised you'd notice anything so ordinary as the house next door having a cat."

"Cats are popular as familiars," Pip said, turning to face him. "And they're connected to the supernatural in a lot of old stories. They don't even have to be black cats, either. In fact—Julian, what are you doing?"

Julian had sat up and had taken hold of Pip's hand. He placed it on his own head. "You're talking too much about cats."

Pip shot Cross an amused smile. He stroked Julian's head. "Am I neglecting you?"

Julian didn't answer the question but leaned against his father in a very satisfied way. "You were going to read me a story."

"Right." Pip heaved himself to his feet. "Bedtime stories it is. Say goodnight to Lord Cross."

Cross smirked at Pip. "What is it tonight? Witches? Egyptian Curses?"

Pip gave him a flat look. "*Treasure Island*, if you must know." He followed Julian upstairs.

Cross smirked again and picked up his book, a celebrated judge's account of various trials he'd been involved in. As he leaned back in his chair, he felt a warm presence against his leg.

"No." Cross moved his leg, scowling at thin air. "I don't like cats. Particularly those who don't have the decency to obey natural laws."

The cat gave him as much care as cats normally did: she leaned against his leg, ignoring him.

"*Shoo.*" Cross waved his free hand in the air, thankful no one was present to witness his behaviour. Could the cat even see him? That was an interesting thought—did the invisibility go both ways?

The cat placed a paw on his knee. A second later, her full weight was in his lap.

"I think not." Cross picked up the cat and deposited her on the floor. "I am not your cushion." He opened his book again. The staff had been preparing the room when Aziza had made her disastrous debut. All the covers had been removed from the chairs and sofas. There were ample comfortable seats for a cat.

But none as desirable as Cross's knees. Wasting no time, the cat once again inserted herself into his lap, butting her head into his hand.

"You are a pest. Why anyone would go to the trouble of preserving you is beyond me." Cross placed his hand on what he presumed was the cat's head. She pressed her whiskers into his fingers. "Unless your presence is a curse." She had, in the short time she had been resident at Trent Street, pushed two vases off their shelves and frightened a housemaid into dropping a third.

The cat rumbled, kneading his paws in a companionable way. She curled up, much as Julian had before bed, and settled down to nap.

Cross waited, but no further insults were forthcoming. He opened his book again, cradling it against the cat's back. Between turning pages, he brushed her fur. "If you have any invisible fleas, your casket is going straight in the fire—I don't care if it is a gift of great sentimental value."

The cat made no reply.

What had that Carruthers chap said her name was? Aziza? It would be interesting to know if a collar placed on her would remain visible—

Cross caught himself. As soon as he convinced Pip to replace the stone, Aziza was resuming her centuries-long rest.

The door opened as Pip stole inside.

"That didn't take long," Cross observed.

"He had a long day," Pip said. "The journey here, all the excitement of the cat, and then our guests tonight. Julian seems quite taken by Captain Candy. He asked me if he could have a glass eye when he's an adult."

"I hope you dissuaded him of that notion." Cross closed his book and placed it on the incidental table beside his chair. "We need to come to some decision about the cat. We cannot keep her."

Pip plopped himself down in the opposite chair. "We can't do anything else. Think of it, Thomas—an actual ghost cat! And one that has been heard and felt by multiple people—who seems to think she is a real cat! There has never been a find like her in, well, that I have heard of, ever!"

"You saw the effect she had on the staff. Even Surplis—who has been remarkably understanding of your collection—"

"Of which Aziza is the gem—the crown jewel!" Pip's eyes shone with a light that never failed to make Cross's heart warm. "You wouldn't ask the Queen to part with the Crown Jewels. Do not expect me to part with my mummified cat."

Cross found it hard to deny Pip anything. Feeling as though he fought a losing battle, he made another attempt. "The Queen's Crown Jewels do not prompt a walkout of her staff."

Pip cocked an eyebrow at him. "While inconvenient, the absence of the staff does lead to some interesting opportunities. We have more privacy than we would normally have."

Cross tried to ignore the stirring of his blood. They were rarely so thoroughly alone, it was true. "The novelty of solitude will wear off by breakfast—which will not be ready for us."

"We can order from a hotel." Pip was unrepentant. He stood, unbuttoning his jacket and draping it over the back of the chair. "We can order all our meals. We'll hardly notice any difference."

Cross rubbed his beard, watching as Pip's nimble hands started work on his vest buttons. "The housework?"

Pip's hands stilled. "I admit you have me there." He paused. "Candy and Carruthers took the cat in stride. Perhaps finding new staff for the townhouse who aren't as nervous as our staff…"

"Candy and Carruthers are the exceptions rather than the norm," Cross said. "You will struggle to find staff willing to overlook an invisible cat."

"Once we replace the stone as Carruthers showed us, she will not bother the staff."

Cross cocked an eyebrow. "Do you think you will be able to refrain from removing the stone?"

Pip looked unrepentant. It was an attitude that suited him well. "You cannot blame me for wanting to become better acquainted with such a marvellous creature."

"Marvellous creature my—"

A rumble filled the air. Aziza nuzzled into Cross's leg, purring in utter content.

Cross placed a hand on her back. He withdrew it immediately.

Too late. "You big softie!" Pip smirked at him. "You have no intention of getting rid of Aziza, do you?"

Cross frowned. "I am indifferent to the cat, I assure you."

"So indifferent you have let her crawl into your lap to make herself at home!" Pip crowed. He knelt by the chair, feeling for the cat and, once he'd discovered her, he stroked her fur. "You like her—admit it, Thomas! You are as pleased with her as I am."

When she was still and not knocking his family heirlooms off their shelves, the cat was more tolerable than anticipated. "I like having a clean house and my meals served on time." Cross squirmed. "Candy intimated that he would not be averse to minding Aziza for us, should her presence prove troublesome."

Pip looked up. "Oh? Carruthers had a word to me of similar import."

"Well?"

Pip looked down. "It seems such a pity. I have wanted a mummy for so long, and now that I have one—and one of such unique interest—it is rather hard not to enjoy it."

Cross reached out, caressing his hair. "Aziza will be in excellent hands. Both Candy and Carruthers seem fond of her, and you can visit them whenever we're in London. As for her care, well, Candy is practically a curator."

"Yes," Pip said slowly. "A curator."

Cross looked up. He knew that tone.

Pip sat back on his heels. "My plans for a phasmatological society have stalled. Why not a phasmatological museum? It could be here in London—a place where my collection might attract the interest of like-minded folk…"

He had to nip this in the bud. Cross scooped up Aziza and set her down on the floor. He took Pip's hand and tugged him to his feet. "Up."

Pip complied. "Don't you want to hear my idea?"

Cross gathered him in his arms. "As our privacy is likely to be limited, it would be a crime to waste it."

The Lord and the Banshee

Death is not the worst thing that can happen.

Thomas Cross, Lord of Foxwood, has received a double blow. The discovery of his terminal illness is followed immediately by the news that his longterm partner Pip is marked for death by the banshee of Connaught Castle. There is no cure for Cross's condition, but there may be a way to save Pip—at the cost of his remaining time.

Recruiting his adopted son Julian to aid him, Cross travels to Ireland to free Pip from the banshee. As each successive encounter with the banshee leaves him closer to death, Cross relies more on a dangerous fairy relic. But the fair folks gifts always come at a price. What is the cost of Pip's safety?

The Lord and the Banshee is the thirteenth in the series of Read by Candlelight gothic novellas featuring an ever-decreasing cast of LGBTQIA characters. Pairs well with chocolate and regret. Preorder now to hate everything.

To be first to read *The Lord and the Banshee*, support me on Patreon. Alternatively, you can preorder it on Amazon. Stay up to date with my news and future releases by signing up to my newsletter.

THE WING COMMANDER'S CURSE

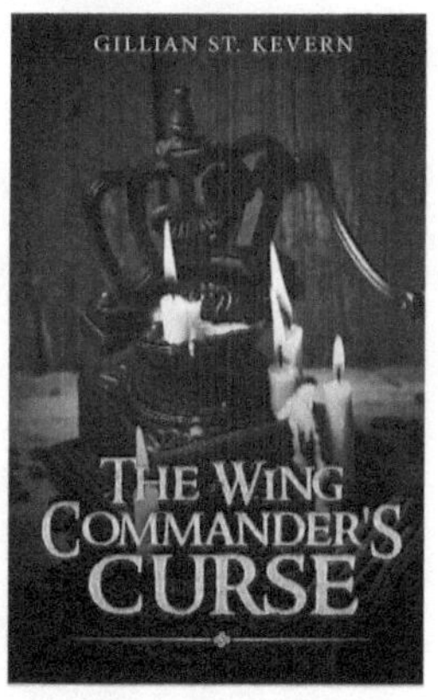

An unbreakable curse.
England overrun by monsters.
Two men locked in a losing battle.

England, 1915.

Jonah Valliant longs for active service, but is stuck making coffee for the local officers. A year ago, the world erupted into magical chaos. No one knows why Britain is overrun by fearsome worms, magical creatures whose gaze turns men to stone, or how to stop them. When Jonah loses his temper with Wing Commander Mallory, he has no idea that picking a quarrel with the wizard may lead to Britain's salvation–or its destruction.

Augustus Mallory carries more than the weight of the war effort on his shoulders. He's the last of the Mallory wizards, feared for their power, arrogance and the dark family curse. Losing his heart to Jonah endangers everything Mallory cares about, but Jonah may possess the key to defeating the worms once and for all. Mallory's only hope: staving off his doom long enough to learn the dreadful truth behind the Quickening.

Sign up to my newsletter for your free copy of The Wing Commander's Curse.

BOOK REC: RIVERS OF LONDON/MIDNIGHT RIOT, RIVERS OF LONDON #1

I was hanging out at my local library last week, and by pure chance happened to see not one but two new books in this series out. I was pretty annoyed—I've been following this series years and was relying on Amazon to tell me when the newest book was out! On the plus side, I now have two new books to read and a third once the library gets it back on the shelf.

This series is a beautiful blend of Police Procedural and Urban Fantasy, with a strong multi-cultural element and LGBTQ representation in later books. I really love the characters and the world building of this series, it is just so good. Definitely check it out!

Note: Midnight Riot is the US title.

"*Midnight Riot* is what would happen if Harry Potter grew up and joined the Fuzz. It is a hilarious, keenly imagined caper."—Diana Gabaldon

Probationary Constable Peter Grant dreams of being a detective in London's Metropolitan Police. Too bad his superior plans to assign him to the Case Progression Unit, where the biggest threat he'll face is a paper cut. But Peter's prospects change in the aftermath of a puzzling murder, when he gains exclusive information from an eyewitness who happens to be a ghost. Peter's ability to speak with the lingering dead brings him to the attention of Detective Chief Inspector Thomas Nightingale, who investigates crimes involving magic and other manifestations of the uncanny. Now, as a wave of brutal and bizarre murders engulfs the city, Peter is plunged into a world where gods and goddesses mingle with mortals and a long-dead evil is making a comeback on a rising tide of magic.

"Filled with detail and imagination . . . Aaronovitch is a name to watch."—Peter F. Hamilton

"Fresh, original, and a wonderful read . . . I loved it."— Charlaine Harris

Read Rivers of London on Amazon.

ACKNOWLEDGMENTS

Very special thanks to my Patreon supporters for their continued encouragement: Jennifer, Julia, Kathleen, Khadija, Lexy, Patricia, SpookMouse, Theanna, Y Lee and Wiebke. It means so much to have you along for the journey.

Another big thank you to Anne and Sera for reading and keeping me on track, Emma B for working her editorial magic and Kevin for his expert proofreading assistance—I would be lost without you and this story would have far more grammatical errors.

ABOUT THE AUTHOR

I realised I wanted to be an author when, as a teenager, I found myself getting annoyed that the characters in the books I read weren't doing what I wanted them to do. Now that I'm a writer, they still don't.

I write a variety of genres, ranging from short and silly contemporary romances to urban fantasy and mystery. My current project is the *Read by Candlelight* series of gothic romances inspired by the works of M R James, J S Le Fanu and the Brontë sisters.

In my non-writing life, I live in my native New Zealand, where I enjoy flat whites, playing pretend with my niece and nephew and trying to keep up with my ever increasing to be read pile. I'm the co-founder of the New Zealand Rainbow Romance Writers.

If you enjoyed *The Dead Letter Office* and want to leave a review, I will be so full of joy, I will make Candy seem restrained.

gillianstkevern.com
info@gillianstkevern.com

CHARACTER GLOSSARY

Suggested by Barb, this is a quick glossary of characters intended to counteract the confusion caused by the fact that the Read by Candlelight series is written and published out of chronological order. This is a work in progress as I intend to update this as I go rather than do it all at once. This is written to accompany *The Dead Letter Office*, and further characters will be added as I have the chance. Get the most up to date version online.

Character Glossary.

Candy, Captain Rudyard.

Retired army officer, now residing in London. Possesses a glass eye, a decent knowledge of antiquities and a very loud laugh. Ha! First appearance: The Dead Letter Office.

Carruthers, Jasper.

Head of the Dead Letter Office, that office of Her Majesty's Postal service concerned with reuniting lost mail with its owners. Fussy, particular, kind, with a marked aver-

sion to argument of any kind. First appearance: The Dead
Letter Office.

Cross, Thomas, Lord of Foxwood.
Landowner of Foxwood Court and much of the
surrounding countryside. A man of uncertain temper, wide
correspondence, and a tragic past. Pip's employer and Julian's
guardian. First appearance: The Secretary and the Ghost.

Leighton, Phillip (Pip).
Secretary and heir to Lord Cross, enthusiastic amateur
phasmatologist and investigator of the occult. Indifferent
health, trained as a legal clerk. Julian's adoptive father. First
appearance: The Secretary and the Ghost.

Westaway, Julian.
Adopted son of Pip, ward of Lord Cross, Patrick O'Con-
nor's godson. Defies explanation. First appearance: The
Disturbance at Foxwood Court.

www.ingramcontent.com/pod-product-compliance
Lightning Source LLC
Chambersburg PA
CBHW032027050726
47590CB00006B/2335